A WITNESS CALLED MARY

THE CALLED
BOOK 9

KENNETH A. WINTER

WildernessLessons

JOIN MY READERS' GROUP FOR UPDATES AND FUTURE RELEASES

Please join my Readers' Group so i can send you a free book, as well as updates and information about future releases, etc.

See the back of the book for details on how to sign up.

∾

A Witness Called Mary

"The Called" – Book 9 (a series of novellas)

Published by:

Kenneth A. Winter

WildernessLessons, LLC

Richmond, Virginia

United States of America

kenwinter.org

wildernesslessons.com

Copyright © 2023 by Kenneth A. Winter

All rights reserved, including the right of reproduction

in whole or in part in any form.

The Called is an approved trademark of Kenneth A. Winter.

Edited by Sheryl Martin Hash

Cover design by Scott Campbell Design

ISBN 978-1-9568661-7-9 (soft cover)

ISBN 978-1-9568661-8-6 (e-book)

ISBN 978-1-9568661-9-3 (large print)

Library of Congress Control Number: 2023902541

The basis for the story line of this book is taken from the Gospels. Certain fictional events or depictions of those events have been added.

Unless otherwise indicated, all Scripture quotations are taken from the *Holy Bible,* New Living Translation, copyright © 1996. Used by permission of Tyndale House Publishers, Inc., Wheaton, Illinois 60189. All rights reserved.

Scripture quotations marked (NASB) are taken from the *New American Standard Bible*, copyright © 1960, 1962, 1963, 1968, 1971, 1972, 1973, 1975, 1977 by The Lockman Foundation, La Habra, California. All rights reserved.

Scripture quotations marked (ESV) are taken from *The Holy Bible, English Standard Version*, copyright © 2001 by Crossway, a publishing ministry of Good News Publishers. Used by permission. All rights reserved.

DEDICATION

To the women in the window
who are faithfully making disciples
among the least reached

~

"Go into all the world and proclaim the gospel to the whole creation."
(Mark 16:15 - ESV)

~

For information about
Women in the Window International
go to:

https://womeninthewindow-intl.org/

CONTENTS

Preface   vii

1. Go in peace   1
2. The tower of the fishes   4
3. A growing enterprise   8
4. My father's little rose   12
5. An opportunity in Tiberias   16
6. Suddenly life changed   20
7. An unexpected turn   24
8. Tormented!   28
9. Set free!   32
10. An unexpected homecoming   36
11. All eyes were on me   40
12. I knew I must go   44
13. Awe and worship   48
14. The Passover   52
15. Jesus has been arrested!   56
16. The unimaginable   60
17. It is finished!   64
18. The tomb   68
19. The Gardener   73
20. That night in the upper room   77
21. Back in Magdala   81
22. A hill outside Bethany   85
23. The Good News spreads   89

Please help me by leaving a review!   94
You will want to read all of the books in "The Called" series   95
"The Parables" series   96
If you enjoyed this story about Mary ...   97
Also by Kenneth A. Winter   98
Also available as audiobooks   99
Scripture bibliography   100
Listing of characters (alphabetical order)   105
Acknowledgments   108
From the author   109
About the author   111
Please join my Readers' Group   112

PREFACE

~

This fictional novella is the ninth book in the series titled, *The Called*. Like the others, it is a story about an ordinary person – a sinner saved by Jesus and called by Him to be used in extraordinary ways. As i've said in my previous books, we tend to elevate the people we read about in Scripture and place them on a pedestal far beyond our reach because of the faith they exhibited. But Mary would tell us she had sunk into the greatest depths until Jesus reached down and pulled her up.

In that respect, her story is much like ours. The apostle Paul wrote, " *Remember, dear brothers and sisters, that few of you were wise in the world's eyes or powerful or wealthy when God called you. Instead, God chose things the world considers foolish in order to shame those who think they are wise. And He chose things that are powerless to shame those who are powerful. God chose things despised by the world, things counted as nothing at all, and used them to bring to nothing what the world considers important. As a result, no one can ever boast in the presence of God."* [1]

And God is still using the foolish, the powerless, those counted as nothing – the ordinary – to accomplish His extraordinary purpose. And He empowers them through His Holy Spirit. He did it in Mary's day – just as He still does today!

There are a number of women named Mary mentioned in the New Testament. This story is about the one called Mary Magdalene. Scripture tells us she was a successful woman; but it also tells us she was under the control of seven demons until the day Jesus set her free.[2]

Afterward, she joined the group that traveled with Jesus and witnessed firsthand the last two-plus years of His earthly ministry. She was one of the few followers who stood at the foot of Jesus's cross when He was crucified. She was one of a handful of women who journeyed to the garden tomb to anoint His body for burial.

She was the first person to whom Jesus appeared after He arose from the dead. She stood on the hill and watched Him ascend into heaven. And she was one of the people praying and waiting in the upper room when the Holy Spirit came upon them.

She witnessed a lot – so there is much she can tell us. Like the other main characters in *The Called* series, Mary had a life before we are introduced to her in the Gospels, and that life continued after we see her name last mentioned. The goal of this story is to help you imagine what her life may have been like in the years leading up to her encounter with Jesus. Most of story leading up to her initial encounter with Jesus is fictional, but i hope you will find it to be plausible and augment the facts we know.

Most of the story from the time she begins following Jesus up until the Day of Pentecost follows the biblical account, with the exception of personal dialogue and snapshots intended to help her tell her story. The book concludes with a fictional view of what her life may have looked like following Pentecost. i pray you find that portion of the story – and the nuggets contained therein – to be plausible as well.

So, i invite you to sit back and join Mary as she shares her story, together with the other characters who have been included as an important part of her journey. You will recognize most of the names in the story from the Gospels. As in all my books, i have added background details about some of them which are not in Scripture, so we might see them as the people they were and not just as names.

i have also added fictional characters to round out her story, and i have given names to those we know existed but remained unnamed in the Bible. They represent the many people who would have surrounded Mary during her lifetime. Included as an appendix in the back of this book is a character listing to clarify the historical vs. fictional elements of each character.

Whenever i directly quote Scripture, it is italicized. The Scripture references are also included as an appendix in the book. The remaining instances of dialogue that are not italicized are a part of the fictional story that helps advance the narrative.

My hope is this book will prompt you to turn to the Gospels and reread the biblical account of Mary's life and, as you do, you will be reminded of the way Jesus transformed the lives of everyone who encountered Him. None of my books is intended to be a substitute for God's Word – rather, i hope they will lead you to spend time in His Word.

Finally, as i have already indicated, my prayer is you will see Mary Magdalene through fresh eyes – and be challenged to live out *your* walk with the Lord with the same courage and faith she displayed. And most importantly, i pray you will be challenged to be an "ordinary" follower with the willingness and faith to be used by God in extraordinary ways that will impact not only this generation, but also the generations to come . . . until our Lord returns!

∼

1

GO IN PEACE

~

When the servant opened the door to receive me, I hastily explained my tardiness. "I have come in response to the dinner invitation my brother and I received from your master. My brother has already arrived, but I fear I am running a little late. Is dinner still being served?"

"Yes, ma'am, it is," he replied, with a quizzical look. "The men are gathered around the guest of honor. But ma'am, there aren't any women among them. Are you certain you were included in the invitation?"

I smiled and answered with confidence. "I am certain that any invitation addressed to my brother was also intended for me. I can hear the men talking; so I will make my way to join them. Besides, I have brought a gift for the guest of honor."

The servant wasn't quite sure what to do as I brushed past him. Though I had not previously visited the Pharisee's home, I was certain I could find my way by following the sound of talking and laughter.

I found the men reclining around a table as they intently listened to the guest of honor speak. But as I made my way to the One I had come to see, each man turned to look at me in surprise. Even my brother seemed somewhat perplexed about why I was there. Once they saw the alabaster jar in my arms, however, they must have assumed I was delivering a present for the Guest of honor, because no one tried to prevent me from approaching Him.

Without stopping to acknowledge anyone, including the host, I walked over to where Jesus was reclining. As I knelt behind Him and opened the jar of perfume, I heard a few gasps of recognition. Several men began to whisper to one another, *"If this Man truly was a prophet of God, He would know what kind of woman this is. She is a sinner!"* [1]

I could not disagree with what they were saying. I knew I was a sinner! But I also knew I was a sinner whom Jesus had set free. As that reality washed over me again, I began to weep. My tears fell on His feet, and I wiped them off with my hair. I began to kiss His feet and anoint them with the perfume. I had come to express my love and gratitude for all He had done for me. I was no longer paying attention to anyone else in the room.

Suddenly I heard Jesus speak to His host, *"Simon, I have something to say to you. A man loaned money to two people – five hundred pieces of silver to one and fifty pieces to the other. But neither of them could repay him, so he kindly forgave them both, canceling their debts. Who do you suppose loved him more after that?"* [2] Simon replied thoughtfully, *"I suppose the one for whom he canceled the larger debt."* [3]

Jesus said, *"You have answered rightly."* [4] Then He turned toward me for the first time and said to Simon, *"Look at this woman kneeling here. When I entered your home, you didn't offer Me water to wash the dust off My feet, but she has washed them with her tears and wiped them with her hair. You didn't greet Me with a kiss, but she has not stopped kissing My feet. You neglected the courtesy of olive oil to anoint My head, but she has anointed My feet with rare perfume. I tell you that her sins – and they are many – have been forgiven, so she has shown Me much love. But a person who is forgiven little shows only little love."*[5]

Most of these men knew me. I had done business with many of them when I was a respected member of the community. And I had even done business with a few of them after that was no longer the case. But even these men had no idea just how far I had fallen. None of them, including my brother, knew the full extent of my pain and despair.

But Jesus did! He had seen me for who I was. And yet, He had not rejected me, and neither had He abandoned me. He had walked through a crowd of people to come directly to me. That's what gave me the courage to walk through this crowd of men and go directly to Him.

He had been the first person in a long time to look at me with compassion instead of contempt. Part of me had wanted to flee from Him that day. I knew from that first moment that He was a righteous Man. I knew I was unworthy of His compassion. But He had looked me in the eyes instead of diverting His gaze – and that was something no one had done in a very long time.

When He spoke to me that day, He was not harsh; rather, He spoke with an authority I had never before experienced. He saved me from the miry pit in which I had imprisoned myself. But in a single moment, He set me free. He made me whole. He gave me a new life.

And now, as He reached down and gently raised my face to look up at Him, He smiled and repeated the words He had said to me earlier that day. "Mary, *your sins are forgiven. Your faith has saved you. Go in peace."*[6]

∽

2

THE TOWER OF THE FISHES

～

No one can recall when Magdala was actually established along the western shore of the Sea of Galilee. Locals say that long before the village sprang up, the waters offshore were already known as one of the most bountiful fishing sites. Native fishermen still boast that Jehovah God favors that part of the sea, and the fish there reproduce more quickly and bountifully than anywhere else.

In fact, it rivals the waters off Bethsaida on the northern shore for the largest concentration of fish. The sea's coastline makes a slight indentation in both locations, creating natural harbors that serve as excellent breeding grounds. The name Magdala means "tower," and some say the location's original name was Magdala Nunayya, meaning "tower of the fishes."

Eventually, a few fishermen and their families established their homes on the shore of this profitable site. More soon followed, and a village was birthed. The fishermen concluded each day with a five-mile journey north by sea to the closest fishery in Capernaum. They sold their daily catches to a merchant named Shebna, who salted and dried the fish for export to distant cities. Although the fishermen would have preferred a fishery much closer, most decided it was more important to be near the source of their income and settled in Magdala. As a result, the village soon became the home to over 200 fishing boats.

As Magdala was becoming established, my grandfather, Johanan, was already a successful young merchant living in Beth She'an, south of Magdala along the Jordan River. The entire region became part of the Roman republic the year Johanan was born. As he grew up, he witnessed the republic's ever expanding imprint on the region. By the time he reached adulthood, Johanan was firmly entrenched in the flourishing trade in and around Beth She'an. He bought and sold products produced in the region and exported them along the growing number of trade routes created by the republic.

Shrewdly, he continued to look for greater opportunities. Though the villages on the western shore of the Sea of Galilee did not enjoy the benefits of Beth She'an – such as an amphitheater, a hippodrome, or a burgeoning cardo (main street) – they had much more to offer an enterprising merchant like Johanan. That region was a growing source of products he could export – not only from the sea, but also from the fertile land along its shores.

Herod the Great had recently begun construction of his palatial city, Caesarea Maritima. It would boast a thriving, manmade harbor allowing trade with places such as Egypt, Rome, and Macedonia. The Romans were finishing a trade road that would connect Caesarea Maritima with Damascus – and from there farther east. And, by the providence of Jehovah, that trade road would pass right by the village of Magdala.

It was a business opportunity my grandfather could not ignore. Johanan packed up his wife, his young son, Jacob, and traveled twenty-two miles to Magdala. When the family arrived, they realized the village was thriving to the point it could be referred to as a city. The synagogue had recently been completed in the center of the city. It was a magnificent structure. The walls of the 1,300-square-foot main hall were decorated with brightly colored frescoes, and inside there was an ornately carved, large stone block featuring the image of a seven-branched menorah.

Johanan acquired a large piece of land just south of the synagogue and hired a carpenter to build a home. Most other homes in the city were one room, but my grandfather needed two rooms since it would also be used for his trade as a merchant. The home was set on a rough stone foundation with a courtyard between the two rooms. The walls were made of mud bricks, then covered with plaster, and the flat roof was constructed with wood and thatch.

Though the house looked plain on the outside compared to their home in Beth She'an, it was quite comfortable. The small windows in each room let in very little light, but with the aid of wooden shutters and woolen matting (added during the colder months), the rooms stayed cool in the summer and warm in the winter. A raised platform at the end of the family's room was used for sleeping and sitting, with cushions and mats adding extra comfort. If the weather became inclement, that room was also used for eating meals and entertaining. Otherwise, those functions took place in the courtyard under an awning.

The second room included a separate doorway from the street to facilitate my grandfather's trade. It contained shelving and tables to accommodate his local trade as well as his export business.

The courtyard was paved with stones and had an open drain in the center. The drain kept the house from flooding during rainstorms and allowed the stone floor to be rinsed off as needed. This was a frequent occurrence since any personal bathing that did not occur on the roof – as well as all meal preparation over an open fire – took place in the courtyard.

Many of the streets in Magdala were too narrow for carts. But my grandfather had the foresight to situate his home in such a way so the pathways to and around it could accommodate the donkey-drawn carts needed to transport the bulky loads coming and going from his shop.

Johanan's trade quickly prospered in Magdala, and he soon became a person of great influence in the city. Sadly, I never met him. He contracted a fever and died in the prime of his life, not yet having achieved all of his ambitious goals. But my grandfather had wisely instilled those plans and his business acumen into my father starting when he was a young boy. So at the age of nineteen, my father took over the responsibility and challenge of leading our family enterprise to even greater heights.

~

3

A GROWING ENTERPRISE

~

$\mathcal{M}$y father did not like to fish. He didn't even like to travel on the sea. But he was an astute merchant just like his father. He and my grandfather had often discussed the need for a fishery in Magdala. Rather than the local fishermen transporting their catches to sell in Capernaum, my father firmly believed, "The profits from Magdalene fish should remain in Magdala."

While my father lacked the knowledge to build and manage a fishery, he knew how to buy and sell better than the best of them. As a result, he always came out on top. It was a skill he learned from his father – and one he eventually passed on to me. So, he went searching for someone who had the expertise to process the fish.

That's how he met Mathias, a fisherman who learned the skill of salting and drying fish early in his career. Mathias had worked for Ishmael, the man who owned the fishery in Capernaum. Though Ishmael paid Mathias well, he never made him a partner. So you can guess what my father did! He immediately offered Mathias a partnership – and the two of them became fast friends and partners from that day forward.

My father then set out to acquire a suitable plot of land along the shore. Ironically, the seller offered to discount the price of the land if my father would make him a partner in the new fishery. But that proposal ran afoul of another one of my father's sayings: "Never settle for short-term gains when you can have long-term profits!" As you might expect, my father chose to pay full price for the land – or at least what my father deemed to be full price. The other man regretted my father's decision for the rest of his life.

The two main ingredients needed to salt fish should come as no surprise – fish and salt. The more than 200 fishing boats docked in our harbor were pulling in an abundance of fish. Salt, however, was another matter. The Sea of Galilee is a freshwater sea, and the salt from the Dead Sea to our south is much too bitter.

Mathias told my father the best salts come from the lagoons of the Mediterranean Sea along the western shore of the province of Sicilia. My father immediately set out to obtain a reliable source of supply from that region and negotiated a deal. His salt supplier would receive a portion of our dried fish, specifically sardines, and my father would receive the salt he needed.

Mathias began to design and build the sheds needed to accommodate the process. The fish were to be prepared for export in one of three ways, each requiring its own unique process. The first way was to ferment the fish, so Mathias set about building vats. A fresh catch would be unloaded into the vats from the fishing boats with alternating layers of Mediterranean salt. The fish would remain in those vats for one to two months before the fermentation process was completed.

This process was also used to produce a profitable byproduct – a popular fish sauce called "garum." It was used to season many cooked foods as well as ferment some wines. Once prepared, the garum was stored and shipped in jars.

The second manner of processing was used specifically for sardines. On average, sardines make up more than half of a fisherman's catch. They were unloaded off the boats and spread out on drying nets raised off the ground to avoid ants. Since sardines are small and thin, they dry quickly. Typically, all moisture evaporates from the fish within two days, making them perfectly preserved and ready for dry shipment.

The third process was reserved for some of the larger fish, which would ultimately find their way onto the tables of the elite. They were kept alive in fresh water from the moment they were caught and expediently shipped in watertight tanks to their destination. Then they were released into piscinas (holding tanks) for storage until the day they were cooked and served as the fresh fish of the day. This process was expensive, and only the wealthy could afford the higher selling price.

To make it more efficient for the fishermen to off-load their daily catches, my father built a stone wharf at the water's edge. He believed if he treated the fishermen fairly and helped lighten their work, they would remain his loyal customers. And he was right. His profitable business began thriving even more. Soon, my father's newest enterprise was flourishing, and Magdala fish was becoming popular on dinner tables from Alexandria to Damascus.

My father prided himself on being a student of the proverbs of wisdom. He began teaching those proverbs to my brother and me while we were still children. One of his favorites was:

Prepare your work outside, and make it ready for yourself in the field. Afterward, then, build your house.[1]

As my father's business continued to prosper, he decided it was time to build his house. Though the home my grandfather built had been appropriate for his day, my father desired something much grander for our family – something more befitting his station as the city's leading merchant. He liked the fact that our homesite was situated on prestigious land just south of the synagogue, so he designed a home to be built on the vacant portion of that land. His intention was that once our new home was built, our old home would become one of his places of business.

He spared no expense in building our palatial home. He incorporated some of the grander elements from Roman architecture that were being seen in parts of Judea and Galilee in the palaces of the Herodians and Romans. Our new home boasted ten rooms, instead of the original two, and the rooms surrounded a columned courtyard with a modern system of drainage and cooking stations. The walls were decorated with brightly colored frescoes, just like our synagogue, and colorful mosaic floors throughout. There was truly no other home like it in the city. As a young girl, I could not imagine anything grander.

~

4

MY FATHER'S LITTLE ROSE

~

*O*ne of the best decisions my father ever made was not a business transaction. It was, however, based on another one of his favorite proverbs.

He who finds a wife finds a good thing, And obtains favor from the Lord.[1]

The Lord did show great favor when my father married a beautiful young woman named Galenka on her seventeenth birthday. She was the eldest daughter of another successful family in Magdala and was well prepared, even at that young age, to carry out the responsibilities as the wife of a successful merchant and city leader, and the mistress over the grandest home in Magdala.

One year later, when I was born, she added the responsibility of motherhood, a role in which she also excelled. My brother, Lemuel, followed two years later. Neither one of us, as we grew, ever felt as if our mother's attention was divided between us. Rather, we always both felt we had her full attention.

However, the same could not be said about our father. Lemuel and I always felt like we needed to compete with our father's business activities for his attention. That is why, as a young girl, I began spending more time with him to better understand those things that seemed more important to him.

As I grew older, it became obvious I took after my father in many ways. He affectionately called me his little rose. He would often say while I was as beautiful as a rose, like my mother, I was also as hardy and resilient as a rose like him. Whenever I was not sitting under the instruction of my tutors, I was at my father's side watching him work. He initially tried to discourage me, saying I would do better to learn from my mother.

But when he eventually realized I would not be dissuaded, he began to explain more about his business affairs to me and even allowed me to help him in small ways. Initially, my job was to carry messages back and forth between him and Mathias down at the fishery. I loved being by the sea at the fishery. Each afternoon, my father made a point of being there when the fishermen arrived with their day's catch. It was obvious he enjoyed haggling with the fishermen over the price he would pay, and it was equally obvious that most of them enjoyed the negotiations as well.

Even though I was young, I could clearly see that the fishermen respected him for being a fair merchant. My father always strove to conclude his negotiations to his advantage, but he was also careful to never take unfair advantage of the fishermen.

"They are my partners," my father once told me. "As long as I am fair, the fishermen will continue to do business with me. After all, we are told in the proverbs of Solomon:

'The Lord demands accurate scales and balances; he sets the standards for fairness,
and righteous lips are the delight of a king, and he loves him who speaks what is
right.'" [2]

By the time I was twelve, my father allowed me on occasion to haggle with the fishermen. Some of the men initially tried to take advantage of my youth and demanded a higher price. But they soon learned I was just as accomplished at bargaining as my father – and just as fair. Not long after that my father renamed the fishery, the Sea Rose Fishery, in my honor. It was one of the proudest days of my life, because I knew my father was beginning to appreciate my contribution to his business.

Around that same time, my father decided Lemuel should start working with him too. Though my brother demonstrated he was a hard worker, he quickly made it known he did not share my enthusiasm for learning about managing the business. To my father's chagrin, Lemuel announced he would always be content to take his direction from our father . . . or me.

I was fourteen years old when our city leaders, including my father, made the decision to expand our synagogue. Our city had grown significantly since it had first been built, and it could no longer accommodate our increased numbers. The other leaders asked my father to oversee the construction.

He immediately put his experience in building our home into practice and hired many of the same carpenters and craftsmen for the task. Though a synagogue by nature is a simple and plain structure, my father still incorporated several elements into its design that set it apart.

The frescoes that adorned the original structure were carried into the new space as well. But my father added decorative elements into the column capitals and door and window lintels that were reflective of temple service. He had the carvers include an image of the lulav (the closed frond of a date palm) and the etrog (a yellow citron). Both elements were used to signify the festival of the harvest, which is called Sukkot.

The completion of the project in record time and at a cost which was well below the initial estimate, earned my father high praise from the other city leaders. His success led to further requests for him to oversee the construction of other important buildings in our city. Sensing another business opportunity, my father decided to formally establish a carpentry enterprise.

That business became so profitable and required so much attention that my father placed it under my supervision when I was eighteen. Though I would be accountable to him, he gave me full authority to direct the endeavor as I saw fit.

We both knew that culturally very few people outside of our family would acknowledge me as the head of the business. I would never be the face of the business, but I would be the brains behind it . . . at least until the day women are finally acknowledged as having the ability to be capable business leaders.

But I took great pride in knowing my father knew I could do it, and we found ways to work around the biases and prejudices we encountered from others. After all, I was my father's resilient little rose.

$\sim$

5

AN OPPORTUNITY IN TIBERIAS

~

I was driven by the same ambition that drove my father – but I knew I needed to be even better because I was a woman. A casualty of that ambition was my social life. Instead, I spent all my time pursuing my education or mastering my business skills.

"You are an attractive and intelligent young woman who would make a fine match for any one of a number of young men," my mother often told me. "It is time for your father to make a marriage arrangement with one of the other leading families in our city. You are not getting any younger, and soon those families will think you're not interested."

"That's because I'm *not* interested," I replied. "You are an excellent wife and mother, devoted to the welfare of her husband and children. But I am not like you, Mother. I am much more interested in furthering the business my grandfather and father have built. I don't have the time or inclination to live out my days as a wife or mother."

My mother attempted to enlist my father's help in talking some sense into me, but he saw my resolve. Though he cautioned me that my choice could lead to a lonely life, I told him, "Father, I desire so much more. You know that! If the right man comes along, who is not threatened by my ambition and has similar dreams, then I will consider him. But you know as well as I do there are not many young men like that living here in Magdala, if any."

It was soon thereafter that Lemuel became betrothed to Leila, a beautiful young woman from another elite family in Magdala. They were perfectly matched. I could not have been happier for them. My mother soon became preoccupied with plans for their wedding feast. And, gratefully, conversations about my own marital status occurred with less frequency.

In the meantime, exciting opportunities were developing on the business front. When Herod the Great died, the Romans divided the regions he had ruled on their behalf. His son, Herod Archelaus, had ruled Judea and Samaria for ten years until he was replaced by a series of Roman prefects. The rule over our region, Galilee, had been given to another of Herod's sons, Herod Antipas.

Since the Roman prefects now lived in the palace his father had built in Caesarea Maritima, Antipas decided that he, too, must build a world class city here in Galilee to be the site of his capital. Galilee does not border on the Mediterranean Sea, and the only body of water of any consequence within its borders is the Sea of Galilee. So, Antipas chose to build his city on its western shore, just a few kilometers south of Magdala.

He elected to follow his father's politically savvy example of naming the city after the current Roman emperor. Thus the city was called Tiberias – and it was to become the jeweled city of the region. No expense would be spared, and it would become the major port city on the Sea of Galilee. In fact, Antipas decided the sea would now be called Lake Tiberias – though few people would ever refer to it by that name.

There was no question that the creation of such a city would bring economic prosperity to all the cities that surrounded it. The capital city would require great quantities of Magdala fish, so the business of the Sea Rose fishery would boom. But I also saw other profitable opportunities the new city would provide.

"Father, our new provincial capital city will require magnificent buildings that reflect its power and greatness," I said. "Though Herod Antipas has chosen to oversee the construction of his new palace himself, many other buildings will need to be built. Would you permit me to pursue the possibility of our becoming the builder of those structures in the new city?"

My father also saw the potential and supported my effort without reservation. I knew that in order to obtain Herod Antipas's approval, I would need to utilize Lemuel as the face of our enterprise. I prepared him and scripted him for each meeting. When the time came to meet with Herod and his council, my father represented us, with Lemuel by his side. Lemuel performed confidently, as of course did my father, and we were successful in our efforts.

Now that we had Herod's approval, our venture began. I hired all the skilled carpenters and artisans we were not otherwise engaging in Magdala, and I even enlisted a few others from Caesarea Maritima. At one point, we simultaneously had ten building projects underway in the city. We no longer needed to seek out new opportunities in Tiberias, we were the ones being sought after.

My life couldn't have been better – or so I thought. My father respected my ability and saw me as his peer. I had always measured my self-worth based on the amount of attention I received from my father – and it had never been greater. Though my abilities were not being recognized, except by my family and a few close friends, I remained confident that would change over time.

My mother was no longer asking me about my intentions to marry. She appeared to accept my decision to remain a successful single woman in a society that didn't know what to make of someone like me.

Yes, my life was just the way I wanted it to be – and I imagined it would only get better.

～

6

SUDDENLY LIFE CHANGED

~

I awoke with a start. Was that a woman's scream? I bound from my bed and ran to my doorway. The scream had now turned into a wail. It was coming from the direction of my parents' bed chamber. What was wrong? What had happened?

As I entered their room, I saw the silhouette of my mother illuminated by the stars in the sky. I quickly made my way toward her. Hearing me, she haltingly gasped, "He's dead! Your father is dead!"

I looked down as he lay peacefully on their bed. My immediate reaction was that he was just sleeping soundly, and my mother had become confused. I placed my right arm around my mother's shoulder in an effort to calm her, while I placed my left hand on my father's forehead.

I instantly pulled back my hand. His forehead was cold to the touch. I leaned down to see if he was breathing. He was not. I turned to look at my mother. "He's gone," she sobbed. "He was fine when we came to bed," she continued through tears. "But I was awakened a few moments ago, and I instinctively reached out to touch him. His skin was cold, and I knew he was gone."

We dispatched a servant to alert Lemuel who lived nearby. He and Leila arrived at the same time as the physician we had summoned, who confirmed what we already knew. He told us my father had died peacefully. His heart had apparently simply stopped beating.

As morning dawned, the news of my father's death quickly spread throughout the city. We were soon surrounded by friends and neighbors who mourned with us and ministered to us in our time of grief. The rabbi and some of my mother's dearest friends took charge and made arrangements for my father's burial later that day. Soon, the aroma of food being prepared, combined with the sweet fragrance of myrrh and spices used to prepare my father's body for burial, began to waft through the air.

Throughout the seven days of mourning that followed, I never gave a thought to our family's business endeavors. I knew Mathias and the others would keep everything operating smoothly. My father and I had selected qualified men to assist us, and they were quite capable of managing the day-to-day needs.

During that time, I did, however, consider what needed to happen next. My father and I had often discussed putting a plan in place for how the enterprise would continue after he was gone, but we had both believed those days were still a long way off. But now those days were here, and we needed a plan.

On the eighth day, my mother, brother, and I found a quiet spot away from the extended family and friends still gathered in our home. We needed to discuss some private family matters.

Lemuel was the first to voice what we all already knew. I was better suited to lead the enterprise. But we also knew the harsh reality that women simply do not run businesses. Their role is to keep the house and quietly support their husbands. No one would do business with us if I publicly took a leadership role. Even the carpenters and craftsmen had seen me as a support to my father. Only a handful of trusted workers knew the reality. The rest would not respond well to taking direction from a woman.

Fortunately, my father had a son who could take over the business – at least publicly. So, we all agreed that Lemuel needed to be the public face of our business, but he would take his direction from me. I would be seen in a support role to him, just as I had been to our father.

But we were also aware that an additional change needed to occur. As our opportunities for trade continued to expand across the Roman empire, we had become increasingly aware that bias and prejudice were not only directed toward women. We had experienced reluctance in some circles in Asia, Macedonia, and Europe to do business with Jews.

My mother was a Hellenistic Jew. Her ancestors had migrated to Galilee from Macedonia. As was common, she and my father had chosen to give both of their children two names – one being Hebrew and the other Greek. My Greek name is Cassandra, which interestingly enough means "the one who shines and excels over men." Lemuel's Greek name is Adrianus, meaning "born of the sea."

We agreed that Lemuel needed to begin using his Greek name in order for us to gain entry into some of those new opportunities. We knew that once we were successful, our products and service would keep us there. And we were correct!

Though I knew my name could not be publicly associated with anything we did, I got an idea one day regarding our carpentry enterprise. As my father's "rose," I was going to add my "personal" signature to every building we built and every venture we started. Through Adrianus, I instructed our craftsmen to carve a unique rosette into the cornerstone of every building we constructed. The rosette consists of six petals that project from the center of the circle, surrounded by six identical petals that form the perimeter.

My father and I had often talked about the fact that Jehovah God is the greatest builder of all. He created everything from nothing in a matter of six days. I designed the rosette as a picture of God's creative work. The six inner petals represent the six days of creation. The six outer petals represent the six major elements of His creation: light, water, land, plants, animals, and humans – created in His image. In my mind, by affixing this personal signature, I was not only gaining subtle recognition for myself, I was also giving glory to God.

The rosette soon became recognized as the symbol of our quality work. Increasingly, we were approached by customers who wanted the prestige of having our rosette displayed on their new buildings. And it soon became the public symbol for all of our businesses. My face was now being seen . . . even though very few knew it was me.

～

7

AN UNEXPECTED TURN

~

*a*s the years passed, it became obvious to my family and friends that I was not going to marry. I did not need a husband to provide for me, and I knew marriage would only complicate our family's business arrangement. Though in the solitude of night, there were times I felt lonely, the rest of the time I was too busy enjoying my success. I didn't want to compromise my pursuit in any way. To be honest, I wanted to be even more successful.

One day while I was evaluating the progress on several of our building projects in Tiberias, an old woman approached me. She was obviously below my station in life. She had a distant look in her eyes, and her speech was erratic. But she was telling me things about myself that no one else knew, including the fact I was secretly leading our family's business. She knew my ambitions. She knew my continuing sorrow over the death of my father. She knew of the resentment I harbored toward a society that marginalized the contributions of women. She knew about the public approval for which I longed. She told me she could help me achieve those desires.

I should have just kept walking and not paid her any attention. But I was curious to see how she could help me. So, I accompanied her to her hovel in a part of Tiberias I had never visited. I was a strong woman, but on that day, she caught me in a weak moment. It was as if she knew just what to say to convince me to do something that, on a different day in a different place, I never would have agreed to do.

As we entered her darkened shanty, my eyes were immediately drawn to the symbols that hung on her walls. Several of them were stars – a couple with five points and a few more with seven. Other symbols were less descriptive. I had never seen any of them in Magdala nor anywhere else I had visited.

I also felt a palpable presence beginning to overpower me. I turned toward the woman and asked, "Is there someone else in here with us?"

"No, dearie," she replied. "It's just you and me. Why do you ask?"

"Because I sense another's presence – either someone . . . or something," I answered.

"Then in that case, I will most certainly be able to help you," she said, without giving any further explanation.

As my eyes adjusted to the dim light, I was able to make out a simple room with stark furnishings. Everything appeared disheveled, much like the woman herself. There were a few blankets and pillows on the floor on which to sit or recline. A few handmade tables held various metallic objects, unlike anything I had ever seen.

The woman told me to sit down while she made us both a cup of tea. By this point, I knew I didn't want to stay there. I wanted to get out from under the oppression I was feeling.

"But I can help you, dearie – just as I promised. We'll sit down over a nice cup of tea. Everything will be fine, and you will have all the answers you are seeking."

Today, I know it was the Spirit of God prompting me to leave that place, but at that moment my curiosity took control over my mind and my heart. I sat down on one of the pillows and considered what she had already told me about myself.

Within moments she was sitting across from me as we sipped our tea. As I listened to her speak, her voice gradually became more hypnotic and soothing. She continued to assure me I could achieve everything I ever desired – and deserved. The attainment of every one of my selfish ambitions was within my reach.

She convinced me my father would want me to have it all, as well – and perhaps, it was his spirit who had led me to her. "Your father only wants the best for you," she said, "just as he always has. It's all within your reach. All you need to do is let go. Allow the presence you sense around you to come within you. Only then will you experience the fulfillment and success you desire. You have achieved many things on your own, but with the power that this presence offers, you will be invincible!"

In that moment of weakness, I succumbed and opened myself up to the spirits she promised me would bring fulfillment and joy. I sensed a surge of emotion and power as those evil powers entered into me. The moment of their entry was invigorating, and for a brief time, there was no question I felt invincible.

As I prepared to leave, the old woman extended the palm of her hand, saying, "What will you give to an old woman who has now given you the power to achieve everything you have ever wanted?"

Naively, I had never even considered the fact she had done all of this for money. But the way I was feeling at that moment, I believed anything that I gave her would be but a pittance in comparison to what she had given me. I reached into my bag and gave her all that I had. The corners of her mouth turned upward as she saw the amount I was placing in her palm. I had not yet realized I had sold my soul and rewarded her for the privilege. I exited her hovel prepared to conquer the world.

But it didn't take long for me to discover the demons within me had taken full control. I was not their host. I was not their mistress. I was their prisoner. The world around me quickly became very dark.

By the time I returned to Magdala, the oppression I felt was no longer contained, it consumed me. It controlled my every action and my every thought. There was no longer any joy, only agony. There was no longer any satisfaction, only desperation. There was no longer any ambition, only resignation.

I pled with the demons to leave me. I told them they were no longer welcome. I told them I no longer wanted them inside me. But in response, all they did was laugh at me.

∽

8

TORMENTED!

~

"What has happened to you?" my mother asked shortly after I arrived back home.

I was too ashamed to admit what I had done, so I replied, "Nothing has happened. Why do you ask?"

"You don't seem like yourself," she answered. "You normally are excited when you return from Tiberias, encouraged by all that you have seen. But today, you seem ill-tempered and easily agitated. Adrianus and I are both concerned that something disturbing occurred while you were away. Is there anything you'd like to tell us?"

"No," I answered curtly. "Nothing occurred that hasn't always been the case. I'm just tired of being overlooked and unrecognized for all I have accomplished in Tiberias. I'm tired of having all the credit and respect for my ideas and my decisions given to Adrianus – or even father, when he was alive. It's not fair, and I'm not going to put up with it any longer!"

"Mary, you know your brother and I – as well as your father, when he was still alive – have always respected the skill and ability Jehovah God has given you to lead our family's business affairs. It has been your idea for us to function in this way since the death of your father. I, too, wish you could get the recognition you deserve, but the world will have to change before that is the case. But what I don't understand is what happened today to cause you to become so angry about it?"

"Today?" I shouted. "It has nothing to do with today! You don't understand because you don't have the gift and abilities I have. You have never had to hide who you truly are. I am so much more talented than you, and Adrianus, and everyone else! It is time for all of you to acknowledge it! I will no longer be silent about it!"

My mother was stunned, and I saw the pain in her eyes. I had never spoken to her in such a disrespectful way. I had not even meant what I said. The words coming out of my mouth were not mine.

Adrianus walked into the room just then, having heard my last remarks. "What has come over you, Mary?" he demanded.

"Nothing has come over me!" I screamed. "The days of my sitting quietly by while you take all the credit for my work no longer exist. You have no right to correct me. From now on, you will simply do as I say – and be thankful for the privilege. Without me, the world would see you for the incompetent fool that you are!"

I saw the hurt and the pain my words inflicted on my brother. My brother is, and always has been, a gentle soul who did nothing but encourage me and support me. And now I was crushing his spirit with my words – words that he did not deserve. And I knew the source of those words.

For a fleeting moment, I was able to seize control of my mouth and my body. "Adrianus and mother, I am so sorry!" I cried out as I ran from the room and out onto the street. Though my brother and mother knew something had happened, they had no idea what. But they feared the worst – and they were right. The voices inside me were tormenting me and they would give me no peace. I had opened myself up to a power and a presence I did not understand, and I quickly realized I could not rid myself of them.

Over the next few days, my outbursts became much worse. My mother and brother tried to calm me, but to no avail. The more they tried, the worse my behavior became. They had no idea what was causing it, but even if they had, they were powerless to do anything about it. The demons were now in full control of my body and my actions. I had become an observer looking out from the prison in which I was confined.

Eventually my mother and brother had to banish me from my own home due to my violent and abusive behavior. I could see their anguish and heartache in making that demand, but their own safety required it. My rampages were no longer a secret within our home. My anger and vitriol were becoming well-known throughout the city. Once one of the most respected women in our community, I was now becoming one of the most despised.

One day, as I was walking in the city, I encountered Simon the Pharisee. Though he had never shown me the courtesy I had at one time deserved, he now made a point of showing me his disdain. He looked at me with disgust and hatred. He turned to those who were walking with him and, pointing a finger at me, said, "This woman is of the devil! For years she has tried to wile us all with her cleverness and savviness. But now we see her for who she truly is. No one in this city is to have any contact with her." He concluded his remarks by shaking out the pleats of his cloak and then hastily walked away.

From that point on, I lost all control of myself. I sought shelter in the caves outside of the city. My body became battered and bruised by injuries I inflicted upon myself. I was in complete agony. I lost all dignity. I even tried to overcome the pain and sense of isolation through immoral behavior.

But nothing helped! The demons inside attacked me every moment of every day. I had become an outcast and my disheveled appearance now completely masked the beauty I had once possessed. My selfish ambition had led to the destruction of everything I once valued. The beauty and wealth I had once possessed had been insufficient to spare me from the evil I had brought upon myself. I had forfeited the blessings given to me by Jehovah God in exchange for alienation and separation.

The petals of the rose had withered and fallen away. There was nothing left on my father's bloom. All hope was gone. My only consolation was that my father had not seen what I had become. There was no one to whom I could turn. There was no one who could take away my pain. There was no one who could rescue me from my captivity. The only solution was to kill myself.

I started to plot my death in such a way that my demons would not be able to foil my attempt. I had learned that though they controlled my body and attacked my thoughts, they could not read my thoughts. They did not know what I was thinking unless I voiced those words out loud.

So I began to design a plan that would be the most important I would ever conceive. It would free me permanently from their captivity.

∾

9

SET FREE!

~

*A*t first, I considered throwing myself off the highest rooftop in Magdala, but I decided someone might attempt to stop me. Then I considered jumping off the highest ledge surrounding the caves that now served as my home, but I could not locate a height that would assure me of my death when I fell. And the last thing I wanted was to become paralyzed from a fall, leaving me incapable of escaping my demons.

I decided my best option was to drown myself in the sea. I would need to wear a garment that would hold enough weight to carry me to the bottom of the sea. I would quickly walk into the water before the demons realized what I was doing. They would fight me once they knew. It would require all the strength I could muster.

I can't tell you what day it was. All the days now looked the same to me. But it was late in the afternoon. The fishing boats were all docked, and the fishermen were in their homes enjoying their late afternoon naps. I walked by the boats closest to shore looking for a garment that had been left behind by one of the fishermen.

I soon discovered one that would serve my purpose. The demons probably thought I was just stealing an article of clothing as I often did. I waded out to the boat, took the garment, and made my way back to shore.

I put on the garment and began to fill it with rocks. When I had added what I considered to be a sufficient weight, I turned to make my way out into the water. But as I did, I saw two men walking nearby along the shore. I knew they would try to stop me, so I turned back and hid in the trees and underbrush.

The men stopped right in front of me and stood there for the longest time. I could not tell if they had seen me. But as I waited for them to walk away, I saw a large group of people walking along the shore from the north. They appeared to be heading to Magdala. The two men who had been standing in front of me walked on. But I decided to continue to hide until the approaching group passed by.

As they got closer, I could see that one Man appeared to be the Teacher of the group, and the others were His followers. Even from a distance, I could see the Man was looking my way, as if he were looking right at me. But surely that wasn't the case. How could He possibly know I was there?

But the closer He came, the more certain I grew that He *was* looking at me. The demons inside me were becoming agitated. I had come to learn their different emotions, but I had never sensed this one before. They were afraid! For some reason, the demons were fearful of this Man!

The Man began walking directly toward me. My first instinct was to shed my outer garment with the weights and run. I, too, was fearful. But I decided if the demons feared Him, perhaps I should see what He wanted.

I stepped out of the brush into plain view. The Man was looking at me with eyes that seemed to penetrate my soul. He wasn't staring at me like other men. It wasn't a look of curiosity, disdain, or fear. To my astonishment, His was a look of compassion!

Part of me still wanted to flee. Part of me wanted to attack Him. But part of me was curious. When He was standing just six feet away, He stopped and looked into my eyes. Suddenly my body began to convulse, and I fell on my knees in front of Him. The demons cried out, "What do you want with us, Jesus, Son of the Most High God?"

The demons knew this Man – and feared Him!

The Man replied, "Come out of this woman, you unclean spirits! I cast you into Sheol to await the day of your judgment! Leave this woman and be gone!"

No sooner had He spoken than I completely collapsed at His feet. After a few moments He gently reached down, took me by the hand, and said, "Mary, arise, for you have been set free!"

In an instant the demons were gone! Those who had held me prisoner for these past months had fled! On the day I had planned to die, I found freedom instead! I cannot begin to describe the flood of emotions that washed through me: a mixture of relief, joy, peace, and gratitude. A weight I had been carrying without any hope of escape had suddenly been lifted off me.

And somehow, this Man knew my name. He had called me Mary. He had known the demons were within me. And He somehow had the authority – and the ability – to cast them out. As I stood to my feet, I looked into the eyes of the One who had just set me free. I saw His compassion, but I also saw His authority. This Man was my Savior. He had released me from my prison. He had done what I could not do – what no one could do!

I did not deserve to be saved. I had imprisoned myself due to my own foolish decisions and selfish ambition. I alone was responsible for what had happened to me. And yet, despite all of that, He had saved me. He was more than my Savior; He was now Lord of my life. He had rescued me. He had freed me. He had cleansed me. I owed Him everything.

I knew He had not rescued me so I could return to my former life pursuing my own ambitions. All of those ambitions had been washed away at the same time the demons were cast away. I was a new person. It was as if He had planted me anew. I was now to be His rose . . . blooming for His glory! I knew immediately I would follow Him wherever He led.

He told me His name was Jesus. He gently instructed me to return to my home and tell my mother, brother, and everyone I encountered that God had shown His mercy on me today. He assured me that those who have been set free are free indeed. And I knew His words were true!

~

10

AN UNEXPECTED HOMECOMING

~

*W*hen I arrived home, my mother and brother were startled to see me. They remained at a safe distance and asked me why I was there. I told them how a Man named Jesus had set me free! He had done what no one else could. They could see a change in my countenance and slowly approached me.

My mother began to cry, as did I, followed soon by my brother. We awkwardly moved closer to one another, not quite knowing what to do. However, within moments all awkwardness disappeared and we embraced, rejoicing in the fact that the Mary we had all once known had returned.

They had never truly understood why I had suddenly acted the way I did. They knew something had taken possession of me – but they did not know how or why. I proceeded to explain what I had done on that fateful day many months earlier in Tiberias. I told them how my selfishness had led to my captivity.

"I cannot solely blame the demons for my actions," I admitted. "I am responsible for inviting them into my life. And as a result, I am responsible for all the mean and ugly things I have said to you. I am the one to blame for my vile actions toward you. I am guilty of the disrespect I showed you. Please forgive me."

At that point, the flood of tears returned – first to me, and then to my mother and brother – flowing like a river of cleansing. We again embraced and this time we held onto one another, thanking God for this miracle. I can't tell you how long we stood there hugging, but I will tell you that we all felt as if a heavy weight had been lifted off of us. Jesus had not only set me free that day; He had also set my mother and brother free.

I told them I needed to find out more about this Man. He had saved my life, and I knew I would never be the same. Yes, I was no longer under the bondage of the demons, but even more than that I knew I could never return to my life the way it had been before my captivity. That decision was not because of what I had done to destroy my reputation; more importantly, I knew I now had a greater purpose – and that purpose had everything to do with Jesus. I needed to go find Him and thank Him.

My mother told me before I did anything else, I needed to bathe and change out of my ragged and filthy clothing. I was still wearing the fisherman's cloak as my outer garment. Underneath the cloak, my other clothing was tattered and torn. That was the first time I had seen my reflection in many months. I barely recognized myself. I was extremely thin and bony, haggard and drawn. What clothing I had was simply hanging off my frame. My eyes were set deep within their sockets. My hair was matted like a bird's nest. The luster of the rose had unquestionably faded away.

My mother tenderly helped me bathe, then patiently and gently brushed my hair. I had forgotten what it felt like to be clean. Once the dirt was gone, I could more clearly see the bruises and scratches I had inflicted on my body. Those would not wash away, but I knew time would heal them.

My mother set out one of my finer tunics and cloaks for me to wear. "Thank you, Mother, for your care and attention," I said. "But I would like to wear something simpler. When I go to find Jesus, I am not seeking to impress Him with my finery. He has known me at my worst. I simply want to go to Him as His servant."

My mother graciously exchanged the clothing for a simpler selection and I put those on. "I have no idea where to look for Jesus," I told her.

Just then a messenger arrived at our door, delivering a note for my brother from Simon the Pharisee. Adrianus read the message aloud: "Jesus of Nazareth is joining me as my guest for dinner this evening. You are invited to join me as well."

Even though I had become an outcast, I was grateful to learn that my brother had been able to maintain his position of importance and influence in the city. But I was even more grateful to know exactly where I could find Jesus. I would go to Simon's home and present myself before Jesus.

"Mary, I do not know how Simon will receive you," Adrianus began cautiously. "I seriously doubt he has invited any women to this gathering. I have never known him to do so, and this dinner will be no exception.

"He also has made his opinion of you very clear to the entire city. He has told everyone to treat you as an untouchable – and until today I would have agreed with him. The three of us know you have been transformed, but he will still see you as a demon-possessed outcast. He will not allow you entry into his home, let alone anywhere near his special guest."

"I completely understand, Adrianus," I replied. "But I sense that I am supposed to go and see Jesus there. I do not know for what purpose, but I sense in my spirit that I am to go there and see Jesus this very night."

"Sister, you have always been wiser than I am – at least until these most recent months. If you believe that is what you are supposed to do, I will not stop you. However, I believe it would be wise for us to go to Simon's home separately."

"You are the invited guest, Adrianus," I said. "It is appropriate for you to go alone. I do not want to do anything that threatens your station of leadership in the city. For these many months, you have not known my comings and goings. To those who are gathered there at Simon's, this night need not be an exception. If things go poorly, you can always express your disapproval of what I have done."

"Mary, I will never voice disapproval of you . . . at least any longer," Adrianus replied. "But I do agree that going separately is the wiser course of action. I will do whatever I can to ease your time there."

When the time arrived, Adrianus departed for Simon's home. I took the time after he was gone to reflect on the day and all that had transpired. What could I possibly do to express my thanksgiving to Jesus? How does one thank the One who has given her back her life?

Just then, my eyes fell upon an alabaster jar of perfume sitting on the table. "Yes! That is how one expresses her thanks!" I declared. I picked up the jar and hurriedly made my way out the door.

∼

11

ALL EYES WERE ON ME

∿

*A*s I made my way through the streets to Simon's home, I could feel the stares of passersby. Even though my appearance had changed some, they still knew who I was – and that Simon had declared me an outcast. I watched as they turned to one another to whisper and point.

One man looked at me and said, "Be off with you, woman! You no longer belong here. We are respectable folk, and you are anything but. Get away from us."

I knew that trying to explain anything to him – or any of the others – would be a wasted effort. Besides, I was on a mission to see Jesus. I would not be dissuaded or delayed.

As I approached the gate to Simon's home, my confidence began to ebb. I heard a voice inside me saying this was a mistake. I knew the voice wasn't the demons. They were gone! Was this a voice of reason? Had I been misleading myself to think I should come here?

The voice continued. "You will embarrass your brother and challenge his reputation. And what's more, you will embarrass Jesus. He has come here to enjoy a good meal with a respectable leader. Who are you to interrupt their dinner?"

Though I did not understand it at the time, I now know the voice belonged to the devil. He was tempting me to turn back. He knew that Jesus fully intended for me to be there. The devil would never be able to thwart Jesus. The only way the devil would ever be able to hurt Jesus would be by convincing His followers to disobey Him.

I decided that anything that leads me closer to Jesus is never wrong! So I continued my way into Simon's home.

As I entered the room where they were all dining, I felt the stares and I heard the gasps. But I saw only one person in the room – and that person was Jesus. I knew Adrianus was there somewhere, but I didn't even see him.

When I knelt at the feet of Jesus, tears of joy and gratitude flowed down my cheeks. Those tears and the perfume I had brought were the only offering I had to give Him.

Simon and the others quickly voiced their displeasure about me, and I wondered if the servants would come and take me away from my Savior's feet. But in an instant, Jesus spoke. As I heard His words, I was taken back to what I had heard Him say only a few hours earlier on the shore: "*Mary, your sins are forgiven. Your faith has saved you.*"[1]

My spirit was at peace. I felt safe – safer than I had ever felt. I was at the feet of my Savior, and He would never leave me to fend for myself. He would never abandon me or forsake me. He would never berate me. Yes, He would correct me when I needed correction. And He would not guarantee I would never encounter difficult people or circumstances, but He would always be with me – every step of the way!

The voices of the other men in the room stopped. Jesus tenderly reached down and lifted up my face to look at Him. There were those same compassionate eyes I had seen earlier – eyes that welcomed me – and eyes that assured me everything would be okay. "*Go in peace,*"[2] He said, as He gently lifted me to my feet.

As I walked out of the room, I noticed that no one was staring at me any longer. Each one of them – including Simon and Adrianus – was looking down, convicted of his own sin. They, too, realized they were in the presence of One unlike any other they had ever encountered. He was more than a great Teacher. He was more than a Miracle Worker. His name was Jesus. And just as I had learned earlier that day – at His name every knee will bow!

I returned to my mother's home and relayed all that had taken place. Adrianus returned shortly thereafter. He told us, "After Mary left, the conversation in the room grew silent. Prior to her arrival, everyone had been trying to impress Jesus with their self-proclaimed acts of charity and goodness. A number, especially Simon, had even attempted to convince Him how well-versed they were in the Scriptures.

"Jesus had looked at each one as he spoke without saying a word. But His gaze said everything. It was as if He knew us and was looking into our very soul. He heard what we were saying, but He also knew what we were not saying. I am convinced He knows more about me than I know about myself.

"And I know if I were to be judged by Him, I would be found guilty – guilty of my sin. Yet, I do not believe He came to that dinner to condemn us of our sin, but rather to show us we can be forgiven of our sin. Just as He forgave you, Mary, and set you free.

"Most of the men left Simon's home with their guilt and shame intact. They refused to accept the forgiveness of Jesus. Sadly, the same is true of Simon the Pharisee. But before I left, I asked Jesus to forgive me. And do you know what He said, Mary? He said the same words He had spoken to you. He said, 'Adrianus, your sins are forgiven. Your faith has saved you.'

"Mary, I now understand why you wanted to go see Him tonight – and what's more I think I understand why He wanted you to come to Simon's house. My life – and the lives of a few others – were transformed tonight. And your obedience to what you knew He would have you do played a key role in our transformation. Perhaps your entire journey, including your demonic possession, was permitted by God so we might all be brought to this night. Perhaps God uses even the pain . . . and the scratches and the bruises."

∼

12

I KNEW I MUST GO

$\sim$

Throughout the night, I struggled with what Adrianus told me. Was he correct? Had God permitted even my captivity for His divine purpose? I knew God had not made me become a captive to the demons. I had done that all on my own! But had He permitted me to do so for a purpose greater than myself – fully knowing that one day His Son would find me on the shores of the Sea of Galilee and set me free?

By the time the sun rose, I knew the answer to that question was "yes!" God, in His sovereignty and infinite wisdom, had done just that – for His glory! And if that was true, I could trust Him with anything. There is so much I will never fully understand. But He does, because He's God.

I awoke with one other answer. I knew I must leave and follow Jesus. My brother had stepped in and directed our family's business affairs quite capably during my absence. There was no reason for me to try and step back in. He had proven he was competent and confident to do so – to others, and, most importantly, to himself. My father would have been proud of him.

With that settled, I could leave my home without any reservation and travel with Jesus. Gratefully, I would also be able to use a portion of the income from our successful businesses to help support Jesus and His followers. I said goodbye to my mother and brother, and joined the growing entourage that was traveling with Jesus.

As it turned out, the majority of the twelve apostles were fishermen from Capernaum and Bethsaida. The rest were carpenters, farmers, and one was a former tax collector. There wasn't a Pharisee, Sadducee, or rabbi among them. Though one of them, the youngest one named John, seemed to have a little more training in the Scriptures than the rest.

They were all plain-spoken men whose only distinction was that they were disciples of Jesus. I quickly learned that the fisherman some called Simon, but Jesus called Peter, was the leader of the apostles. He often spoke up when others were silent. And I could tell right away he had a good and tender heart.

In addition to the apostles, there were a number of other men and women following Jesus. Some were His relatives, others were relatives of the apostles, and still others, like me, were people Jesus had touched along His way. One of them, a shepherd named Shimon, had actually seen Jesus in Bethlehem the night He was born. Everyone had a story about how they had met their Savior.

Jesus's mother, whose name is also Mary, traveled with Him as well. But though I always saw Jesus being respectful and honoring of His mother, she did not hold a different place of standing from the other women in the group. We all contributed however we could. A number of us provided money to purchase food for the entire group, as well as the funds for lodging when required. Most of the time we slept under the stars or in the homes of friends Jesus met along the way.

All the women helped with the cooking. The overall group numbered between fifty and a hundred people, depending upon the season. So preparing meals for that many mouths was no small task.

In addition to Jesus's mother, there was a third Mary. She was Jesus's aunt, the wife of His uncle, Clopas. Their sons – the carpenters James (often called the less, because he's shorter than John's brother, James) and Thaddeus – are two of Jesus's apostles. This Mary is slightly older than I am, and I have found that she keeps a watchful eye over Jesus's mother.

The other women include Salome (the mother of the apostles John and James), Joanna (the wife of Herod Antipas's royal chamberlain, Chuza), and Susanna (a widow whose son Jesus raised from the dead). Like I said, everybody had a story, and we all came from different backgrounds; but most importantly, we had one thing in common – Jesus.

The only person I knew prior to following Jesus was Joanna's husband, Chuza. Since he was Antipas's royal chamberlain, I had spoken with him in Tiberias on several occasions in the company of my father and brother. He had been helpful in our attaining Herod's approval to build in the city.

Jesus had healed his and Joanna's son from a critical fever simply by speaking the words, even though the boy was far away from Him at the time. I had actually heard the story from Chuza one day soon after it occurred (before I became demon possessed). But at the time I had not heard of Jesus, so the story did not mean much to me. But now, it had taken on great significance.

I traveled with Jesus for over two years. Each day, I witnessed Him perform miraculous things. I saw him deliver others who were demon possessed. I rejoiced with them as they experienced their release from bondage. I knew what that felt like! I saw Him enable the blind to see, the deaf to hear, and the lame to walk.

One of the most significant miracles I witnessed was the day he raised his friend Lazarus from the grave. We had all been staying in Bethabara for the winter months when Jesus received word from Bethany that Lazarus was sick. Unbeknownst to the rest of us, Lazarus had died even before the messenger arrived in Bethabara that day.

But Jesus, of course, knew. He intentionally remained in Bethabara another two days before He announced He was going to Bethany, to the home of Lazarus and his sisters, Martha and Miriam. No one among us knew why He had delayed or why He was now going to see them. It all seemed too late. And honestly, it had shaken most of us. If Jesus had been unwilling or unable to heal his close friend, what did that mean for the rest of us?

It was the first time I, or any of His other followers, had truly questioned His actions. But our concerns were quickly erased the moment we saw Lazarus walk out of that tomb in response to Jesus's command, *"Lazarus, come out!"*[1]

Through all of His miracles – including my own – and all of His teachings, it became clear He had an authority unlike any other. But, at the moment I saw Lazarus walk out of the grave, there was no doubt in my mind that He was the Son of the Living God!

∾

13

AWE AND WORSHIP

~

*A*bout two months had passed since Jesus raised Lazarus from the dead. Word of this miracle had spread far and wide throughout Judea, Galilee, Samaria, and Perea. Even those who had not previously heard of Jesus quickly learned He had brought a man back to life.

The power of God had not been witnessed like that since the days of the prophets Elijah and Elisha. Jesus was being called the greatest prophet who had ever lived, and many were saying He was the Messiah. We heard that more people were coming to Jerusalem that year to celebrate the Feast of Passover than ever before. And the reason was, they knew Jesus would be there!

It had become increasingly difficult over the years for pilgrims to find a place to stay in Jerusalem during the Passover. Many were forced to lodge several hours away. In prior years we had found rooms in Jerusalem, but this year Jesus arranged for us to stay in the home of Lazarus in Bethany.

The first night we were there, Lazarus's sister Miriam knelt beside Jesus and anointed His head and feet with a sweet-smelling perfume. As soon as she opened the jar, the aroma spread throughout the house. Even those of us assisting her sister Martha in preparing and serving the meal were quickly enveloped in the scent.

It immediately took me back to the night over two years' earlier when I had been the one kneeling at Jesus's feet. I, perhaps more than anyone else, understood the overwhelming depth of Miriam's love and gratitude for what Jesus had done – and for who He was. I was surprised, however, since those sitting around the table were all Jesus's followers, when I heard Judas Iscariot remark, *"That perfume was worth a year's wages. It should have been sold and the money given to the poor."* [1]

Several other apostles then joined him in scolding Miriam. I had not been surprised when I received criticism for doing a similar thing to Jesus – the majority of the men in the room that night had not been followers of Jesus. But this night was different. These men were the closest followers of Jesus, and they were reprimanding this woman for sincerely and authentically worshiping Him.

Just like He had that night for me, Jesus spoke up and said, *"Leave her alone. Why would you criticize her for doing such a good thing to Me?"* [2]

I began to weep. Miriam's actions brought back to the surface the full measure of my love and awe for Jesus and all He had done for me. Several others saw my tears and thought I was remembering the night I had anointed Jesus's feet. And in some ways, they were correct. But it was more than that. Sadly, I feared my love and awe had somewhat diminished from what it had been that night in Simon's home.

And as I looked around at each person in the room, I wondered if that were true of all of us. We had lost our first love due to our familiarity with Him. We, who were sitting there in the room with Him, had forgotten how to worship Him.

"Father," I prayed silently, "help my reverence and love for You and Your Son grow with each day and not diminish. Help it to grow to be as pure and as vibrant as Miriam's expression at this moment. And Father, make that true for each one of us."

As I looked back over the room, I saw Lazarus and Martha hovering over their guest of honor, attending to His needs. Miriam was now quietly kneeling at Jesus's feet, the aroma of the perfume still permeating the air. Judas Iscariot still looked indignant, and the rest of the apostles were now talking about something else altogether. The moment had passed, but I prayed the impact it had made on my heart would not.

The next morning, we followed Jesus as He made His way to Jerusalem. I was walking alongside His mother, Mary. On the outskirts of the city, He dispatched two of His disciples to fetch a donkey and its colt. Mary and I watched with curiosity as Jesus mounted the colt and started making His way into the city. Suddenly people began crowding along His path.

As He drew closer to the city gates, a multitude poured out of the city. I had never seen such a throng of people, and I dare say neither had anyone else. Spontaneously the crowd began to sing and shout, *"Praise God for the Son of David! Blessings on the One who comes in the name of the Lord! Praise God in highest heaven!"* [3]

Mary turned to me and said, "Today this crowd is shouting words that proclaim the same message an angel spoke to me many years ago before Jesus was born:

"Jesus will be very great and will be called the Son of the Most High. And the Lord God will give Him the throne of His ancestor David, And He will reign over Israel forever; His Kingdom will never end!" [4]

The heartfelt expressions and excitement of the crowd continued to build. No one could have stopped them if they tried. It reminded me of Miriam's heartfelt worship the night before – and mine in Simon's home.

Just like those two occasions, however, the moment was met with the sour expressions of naysayers. Several Pharisees indignantly called out to Jesus, *"Teacher, rebuke Your followers for saying things like that!"* [5]

Now, for the third time, I heard Jesus come to the defense of those who were simply endeavoring to express their worship and awe. Jesus replied, *"If they kept quiet, the stones along the road would burst into cheers!"* [6]

At that moment, Mary and I lifted our voices with the crowd:

"Praise God for the Son of David! Blessings on the One who comes in the name of the Lord! Praise God in highest heaven!" [7]

∽

14

THE PASSOVER

~

*O*ur return to Bethany later that afternoon was much quieter than our entry into Jerusalem that morning. The large throng of people was still gathered, though now they looked perplexed. I believe we all thought Jesus was going to make a public declaration when we arrived at the temple. Why else had He chosen to ride the colt and enter Jerusalem through the Eastern Gate – the King's Gate? But instead, He simply walked around the temple courts, prayed, and then quietly left.

When Jesus and His apostles went back to Jerusalem the next morning, the rest of us remained in Bethany. When they all returned that evening, we learned that when they first arrived at the temple that morning, Jesus saw that tables and stalls had been erected in the outer court by money changers and sellers of birds and animals.

Though Jesus had cleared them out of the temple three years earlier, the practice had been resumed that morning. The apostle John expressed his suspicion that the religious leaders had brought them back in order to provoke Jesus. After seeing the crowd's reaction the day before, the religious leaders were undoubtedly seeking to challenge His authority.

None of this, however, appeared to have dissuaded Jesus. After He cleansed the temple, He remained there throughout the day, healing and teaching the crowd. As I think back to that night, He made no mention of the day's events Himself. It was all told to us by the apostles. As the night unfolded, we enjoyed a pleasant time of fellowship around the table – not knowing it would be our last together.

Jesus returned to the temple the next day, which was Tuesday. He again healed and taught just as He always had when He was in Jerusalem. I later learned the religious leaders sent people to question Him throughout the day, apparently intending to confound Him. However, as was always the case, the leaders soon retreated in defeat.

We received word in Bethany late that afternoon that Jesus and the apostles would not be returning that night. Instead, Jesus planned for them to spend the next several nights praying on the Mount of Olives. We were instructed to make preparations for the Passover Seder for Thursday evening. Jesus would meet us at the room in the city where He had arranged for the meal to take place.

The Passover Festival would begin at dusk with the Seder and continue for seven days. In preparation for the festival, all of the leaven was removed from Jewish households. Leaven symbolized corruption, or sin, so for the seven days of Passover we were to eat only unleavened bread. Any leaven remaining in the households on this day was removed and burned.

As we made our way to Jerusalem that day, the pungent odor of burning leaven permeated the air. Every household was busy completing their arrangements. When we arrived in Jerusalem, we received instructions to go to an upper room owned by a tradesman named Yitzhak.

Mary (the mother of Jesus), Salome (the wife of Zebedee), Mary (the wife of Clopas), Joanna (the wife of Chuza), Susanna (the widow whose son

Jesus raised from the dead), and I busily began to make everything ready for the evening using the supplies Yitzhak had provided.

Later in the day, Jesus and the apostles arrived. Before the meal began, Jesus reclined at the table. Looking back, I cannot believe how calm He was. Jesus knew what was about to unfold; and yet, there He was looking completely relaxed. He knew that everything was going to happen according to His Father's plan. So, He rested and renewed His strength for what would soon unfold.

Then Jesus did something that surprised us all. He got up from the table and kneeled before each one of His apostles, washed their dirty feet, then dried them with the towel He was wearing around His waist. A hush fell over the room as Jesus knelt before one man and then the next.

Then Jesus came to Simon Peter, who protested saying, *"Lord, are You going to wash my feet?"*[1]

Jesus replied, *"You don't understand now what I am doing, but someday you will."*[2]

"No," Simon Peter protested, *"You will never ever wash my feet!"*[3]

"Unless I wash you, you won't belong to Me,"[4] Jesus replied.

Then Simon Peter exclaimed, *"Then wash my hands and head as well, Lord, not just my feet!"*[5]

To which Jesus responded, *"A person who has bathed all over does not need to wash, except for the feet, to be entirely clean. And you disciples are clean, but not all of you."*[6]

I did not know what Jesus meant by His last statement. I don't believe anyone did. But before the sun rose again, we would all become painfully aware.

When Jesus had finished washing the apostles' feet, He continued speaking to the men while the women set about serving the meal. I soon saw Judas get up from his place at the table and leave the room. I didn't think much about it at the time. It seemed that he was often going out for one reason or another.

After Judas departed, Jesus took some bread and gave thanks to God for it. Then He broke it in pieces and gave it to us, saying, *"This is My body, which is given for you. Do this in remembrance of Me."*[7]

After supper, He took another cup of wine and said, *"This cup is the new covenant between God and His people – an agreement confirmed with My blood, which is poured out as a sacrifice for you. Take this and share it among yourselves. For I will not drink wine again until the Kingdom of God has come."*[8]

Now as I think back, I understand what Jesus meant when He told us to remember His broken body and His shed blood. But at the time, all I knew was my heart felt heavy as He spoke those words. And I couldn't understand what He meant when He said He would not be drinking wine again until the Kingdom of God has come. This had not been like any other Passover meal we had celebrated together. This time, Jesus was pointing us to what was to come rather than to what had passed.

We all sang a song, and then Jesus and the apostles departed for the Mount of Olives. The other women and I cleaned up after the meal and made our way back to Bethany. None of us could have anticipated what was about to happen.

~

15

JESUS HAS BEEN ARRESTED!

~

*I*t was quite late by the time we arrived back in Bethany and had settled for the night. We were all sleeping soundly when we were startled awake by several men shouting. I immediately headed for the courtyard to see what was happening. Lazarus was right behind me, followed by his two sisters and the other women. We were surprised to find it was several of the apostles who were creating the stir, and we couldn't understand a word they were saying.

"Men, we cannot understand you!" Lazarus shouted. "Please be quiet! And one of you tell us what has happened!"

It took a moment for the men to quiet down, but then James, the brother of John and the son of Salome, began to speak. "Jesus has been arrested! We were all fast asleep in the Garden of Gethsemane when a large mob of priests, temple guards, and Roman soldiers armed with clubs and swords came upon us. Within moments we realized they were being led by Judas Iscariot!

"Judas walked right up to Jesus, and I heard him loudly exclaim, '*Rabbi!*'[1] and greet Him with a kiss. Judas acted as if he hadn't seen Jesus in quite a while and extended the traditional greeting for a respected teacher and mentor. But the action of the crowd was anything but cordial and respectful.

"Then I heard Jesus say, '*Judas, would you betray the Son of Man with a kiss?*'[2]

"Immediately the captain of the guard told the temple guards to take hold of Jesus and arrest Him. When Peter saw what was happening, he drew his sword. A man standing nearby looked ready to swing his club at Jesus or one of us. Peter struck the man with his sword. His blade was true, and he sliced off the man's ear.

"Before anyone else could react, Jesus shouted at us, '*No more of this! Put away your sword. Don't you realize that I could ask My Father for thousands of angels to protect us, and He would send them instantly?*'[3]

"With that, Jesus reached out to the man, touching his ear. Immediately, the man's pain was gone. As he felt his ear, realizing Jesus had restored it, he dropped his club to the ground and trembled before Jesus.

"We all looked at one another. Jesus had just told us not to fight. Even if He hadn't, Peter and Simon the zealot were the only ones among us with a sword. The size of the mob was overwhelming. Obviously, the religious leaders were not taking any chances on Jesus escaping their grasp.

"We were all frightened and in shock. None of us ever anticipated they would send soldiers in the middle of the night to arrest Jesus. We had no idea what was going to happen to Him – or to us. I am ashamed to admit we all began to fear for our own safety, so we abandoned Him and ran in different directions.

"In my haste to get away, I heard Jesus ask His captors, '*Am I some dangerous revolutionary that you come with swords and clubs to arrest Me? Why didn't you arrest Me in the Temple? I was there every day. But this is your moment, the time when the power of darkness reigns. And since I am the One you want, let these others go.*'(4)

"By the time He finished speaking, He was standing alone in the midst of a mob that was there to arrest Him. All of us had abandoned Him. Not one disciple remained – except Judas, the betrayer!"

With that, James and the other men began to wail loudly out of humiliation, fear, and dread for what was happening to Jesus. His mother, Mary, fell to her knees and began to weep. My mind was reeling from shock. How could this be? How could Jesus have permitted it to happen? How could the Father have permitted this to happen?

Suddenly, I knew we needed to find where they had taken Jesus. If His apostles had abandoned Him, He would be alone with no one to advocate on His behalf. We needed a plan. I immediately began to search among the men for Simon Peter and John. But they were not there.

"Where have they taken Jesus?" I asked.

"We would suspect He has been taken to stand before the Sanhedrin," James replied. "But we do not know for certain."

"What has happened to Peter and John?" I asked. "Where are they?"

"We do not know," Andrew answered. "When we scattered, the two of them, together with the shepherd Shimon, ran farther up the mount, whereas the rest of us began to run in this direction."

I looked at Jesus's mother and knew this was more than she could bear. I turned to Mary, the wife of Clopas, and said, "You and I need to go with Mary to find her Son. Surely this will all be settled without Jesus coming to any harm. The religious leaders will most assuredly come to their senses – or if not, the Heavenly Father will intercede on His Son's behalf!

"The Sanhedrin will not be so brazen as to cause any harm to three women, particularly to the mother and aunt of Jesus. We must make our way quickly before any more time passes!"

"I will go with you!" Lazarus declared. "I will use my influence in the city and bear witness to how Jesus raised me from the dead! Surely, they will see their error in what they have done."

It was Philip who interrupted him saying, "Lazarus, you cannot be seen in Jerusalem right now. Rumors have spread ever since your resurrection that the religious leaders have been plotting to kill you as well. Now that they have been so bold as to arrest Jesus, they will not hesitate to arrest you – or worse!"

Martha and Miriam added their caution. "Brother, Jesus did not return your life to you so you might forfeit it just two months later. Heed Philip's words of wisdom. You cannot go to Jerusalem at this time!"

All of us agreed he needed to remain in Bethany, so we three women set off on the journey to Jerusalem.

∽

16

THE UNIMAGINABLE

~

By the time the three of us arrived in Jerusalem, the sun had already risen well into the sky. The people in the streets were all talking about Jesus and the fact that the religious leaders had taken Him before Pontius Pilate. To our horror, some were even saying that Jesus was to be crucified! Certainly they were mistaken!

We soon learned that Jesus had been taken to the Antonia fortress. Why would they possibly be holding Him in that Roman prison? Didn't the Romans know that Jesus wasn't a criminal? What kind of madness had suddenly overtaken Jerusalem?

We made our way to the fortress and encountered John and Shimon outside the gates. They quickly told us what had occurred. After Jesus's arrest, He had been taken to the home of the high priest to stand trial. That mockery of religious law had found Him guilty of heresy, as well as acts of sedition, and sentenced Him to death.

He had then been taken before Herod Antipas as well as the Roman prefect, Pontius Pilate, who had succumbed to the religious leaders' pressure to sentence Him to death on the cross. We could not believe what we were hearing. John had just confirmed that Jesus was to be crucified on a cross! Surely the Father would stop it. Surely all of this madness would cease. If nothing else, the Father would send a multitude of angels to rescue His Son.

Shimon told us he had met the commander of the Antonia fortress earlier that week. "I will send him a message and tell him Jesus's mother is here at the gate," he said. "The other day when I spoke with him, he seemed genuinely concerned about threats being made against Jesus. I will ask his permission for her to see her Son."

We were hopeful until we received this reply:

"The city is in an uproar over Jesus. No one is permitted to see Him. His mother will need to speak to Him as He hangs on the cross."

A few minutes later, a cohort of soldiers exited the fortress. They surrounded three men, each one carrying his own cross. According to Roman law, one who was found guilty and condemned to death was required to carry his cross, or at least the cross beam, to the place of his crucifixion. The third of the three men was Jesus. Mary let out a gasp at the sight of her beloved Son. He was barely recognizable.

His face had been pummeled. He was wearing a crown of thorns thrust into his scalp. Blood was streaming down His face and neck, saturating his clothing, particularly the back of His garment. All three men had been beaten, but it was obvious that Jesus's beating was the most severe.

Given His weakened condition, Jesus struggled under the weight of the cross. The soldiers seized a man from the crowd, whom we later learned was named Simon, and forced him to carry Jesus's cross. None of us knew who he was, but we knew we would be indebted to him for his kindness, albeit involuntary.

The pathway was lined with onlookers. In some ways, it was like a few days earlier when everyone was pressing in to see Jesus riding on the colt. But this time, there were no shouts of praise. Instead, some of the people in the crowd were shouting, "Crucify Him!" But most stared silently, many with tears streaming down their cheeks. Above the noise of the crowd and the sound of the soldiers' whips were our grief-stricken cries as we trailed behind.

At one point Jesus turned back toward us and said, *"Daughters of Jerusalem, don't weep for Me, but weep for yourselves and for your children."*[1] He then briefly bore witness to what would occur in the end times. Even as He was being led to His death, Jesus was speaking as One in authority.

When our procession of death arrived at the place of execution called Golgotha, Simon's task was finished. He was told to leave, but he apparently felt compelled to remain at the foot of the cross. He later told us he felt drawn to Jesus. Something had occurred in his heart as he carried that cross, though he couldn't explain it. He had heard of Jesus the Miracle Worker, but that morning he realized Jesus was so much more. As the other two Marys and I, together with John and Shimon, gathered at the foot of the cross, Simon remained there at our side.

We wept until it seemed we had no more tears . . . and then we wept some more. After a while, Jesus looked down from the cross and, seeing His mother standing beside John, said to them, *"Woman, he is your son. And John, she is your mother."*[2] His eyes were filled with compassion as He honored and completed His responsibility as the firstborn son of His earthly mother.

I was curious why Jesus had not asked one of Mary's other sons – James, Joseph, Jude, or Simon – to watch over her. James, as the next oldest son, would normally have been given the responsibility to care for His widowed mother. But I quickly realized that James and the other brothers had not yet believed in Jesus. They were not like-minded, and He would not entrust His mother to anyone who was not.

It was then I noticed that none of Mary's other sons were there with her at the cross. I knew they had come to Jerusalem for the observance of Passover, so I was surprised they hadn't sought out their mother to comfort her. I didn't know whether they feared retribution because they were family, whether it was due to their unbelief in Jesus, or maybe because they were embarrassed over the way they believed He had sullied the family's reputation.

Regardless, I did know this. As He hung on that cross, with His mother as His only immediate family member present, Jesus entrusted her to John's care.

At noon, a veil of darkness fell across the land. The crowd grew fearful. What had caused the sun to be extinguished in the middle of the day? I heard a man standing near us whisper to the man beside him, "I once heard Jesus say in the courtyard of the temple, '*I am the light of the world. If you follow Me, you won't be stumbling through the darkness.*'[3]

"Could it be that everything He said was true, and everything the religious leaders have said about Him is false? Could their actions to have Him crucified now be causing us all to be plunged into darkness?"

The other man replied, "I do not know! But I am not going to stand here any longer to find out." With that, both men made their way back toward the city. Those in the crowd who had been mocking Jesus did the same. Even the Roman soldiers were unsettled and looked up at the sky in fear.

$\sim$

17

IT IS FINISHED!

~

*N*one of us knew why the sky had turned dark. We presumed it was the Father's sorrow over what was being done to His Son – because it mirrored the sorrow in *our* hearts. We later learned there was a transaction that took place that day between the Father and the Son. It was an exchange for the sins of the world – something that none of us could ever truly comprehend even once Jesus explained it to us. But on the day itself, all we could do was watch in sadness.

As I looked up at Jesus, my mind raced back in time. I pictured Him on the day He freed me from my bondage. I thought of the day He broke the loaves and the fishes and fed the multitude. I remembered His delight as He spoke of the faith of that little boy. I reflected on how patiently He had always answered our questions. I recalled the many times I heard Him laugh, as well as the times I saw Him weep over the destructive power of sin. I pictured Him, just the night before, as He had knelt before His apostles and washed their feet.

Abruptly, my mind went in a different direction. This time it was unbelief. How could the Father permit this to happen to His Son? Jesus is the

Messiah – why hadn't the Father sent a host of angels to deliver His Son and overpower these Roman soldiers? Why was this One who has delivered so many from pain and suffering being forced to endure it Himself?

I was overwhelmed with feelings – heartbreak, anger, helplessness, hopelessness, and even faithlessness. Jesus had become my life and my hope. What were we to do? What was I to do? I could no longer see past the death and agony right before my eyes. Then suddenly Jesus cried out, *"It is finished!"* [1]

I stood by Mary's side as the horror continued to unfold. A soldier thrust his spear into Jesus's side to make sure He was dead. Blood and water flowed from His body. Even after death, they were subjecting my Savior to barbaric cruelty. I embraced Mary as we stood there and wept uncontrollably. Mercifully, the centurion called out to His soldiers that Jesus's body was not to be subjected to any more brutality.

My heart was so heavy I thought it was going to explode. I wanted to be strong for Mary, but I was also walking through my own anguish. I imagined I could hear the voices of the demons celebrating the pain and suffering of Jesus. It must have seemed like a triumph to Satan.

His puppets, the religious leaders, had smugly considered Jesus's death a victory. The threat to their position and power had been eliminated forever. And to a watching world, it was a brutal murder – to many, an injustice. But to the Father, it was the only way His creation would ever be able to cross the sinful divide back to Him.

As I looked up at Jesus's now lifeless body, I cried out, "The Son of God cannot die!" In my spirit, I knew there had to be more to come. But my heart was drowning in grief. I could no longer be strong for Mary. I fell to my knees and wept.

According to our custom, it was the responsibility of Jesus's family and friends to arrange for His burial. But there hadn't been any time for us to even consider this need. His mother and the rest of us had been in shock ever since we heard the news of His arrest. We had never even considered His death a possibility. And His brothers hadn't been seen at all throughout the day's events.

Victims of crucifixion were usually left to be eaten by birds and wild animals or thrown like garbage into the dumping area in the Kidron Valley and burned. But that would not be the case for the Son of God!

Gratefully, His Father had a plan. He had prompted Joseph, the Pharisee from Arimathea, to make the needed arrangements. Joseph went to Pilate and requested the body, even though he knew his action would not be popular with the high priest Caiaphas, his father-in-law Annas, and most of the members of the high council. In fact, his deed would be considered an outright act of betrayal by most of his Sanhedrin brothers.

It was political suicide for Joseph, jeopardizing his position on the Sanhedrin, his influence in the community, and his personal wealth. I admired his courage and strength of character. Joseph provided the newly hewn tomb in which Jesus's body would be laid, as well as the linen cloth with which to wrap His body.

The Pharisee Nicodemus also assisted in the burial. He brought the embalming ointment to prepare Jesus's body. The Sanhedrin would not have looked kindly on his participation either. The two men acted quickly so Jesus's body could be laid in the tomb according to the law of Moses before the beginning of Sabbath at dusk.

Even though Jesus had told us He would rise again, not one of us was watching by faith. We were overwhelmed by grief and never contemplated that possibility. Interestingly enough, the only ones who remembered His promise were the religious leaders.

When they heard Joseph had made arrangements to place Jesus's body in his tomb, they petitioned Pilate to post guards at the tomb entrance. They were fearful we, as His followers, would remove His body and make the claim He had risen from the dead. We hadn't even thought about burying His body, let alone arranging a false resurrection!

Simon, the man who carried Jesus's cross, had stood quietly with us at the foot of the cross in reverence until Jesus breathed His last. Then he, too, fell to his knees with the rest of us weeping. When he saw Joseph and Nicodemus preparing to take Jesus's body to the tomb, he approached the two men. "The soldiers compelled me to carry His cross," he said. "But now I believe God is compelling me to carry the broken body of His Son to His tomb."

Jesus's Aunt Mary and I volunteered to help prepare Jesus's body for burial. But Joseph and Nicodemus told us there would not be enough time for us to get all the spices and perfumes we would need. Joseph gently said, "Delay your preparations until after the Sabbath. Then you can go to the tomb and do so. And in the meantime, stay by His mother's side and console her."

~

18

THE TOMB

∼

*W*e quietly followed Joseph, Nicodemus, and Simon to the tomb in the garden. Though we knew we were being watched, we were grateful no one tried to stop us. Once we arrived at the tomb, Joseph and Nicodemus quickly went about their work.

As the sun was just preparing to set, the three men rolled the boulder back over the tomb's entrance. John announced that he needed to go find Simon Peter. By then, we had all learned Peter had denied knowing Jesus soon after His arrest.

Jesus had told Peter the night before that he would deny Him three times before the rooster crowed the following morning. Peter had, in his typical fashion, argued that he would never deny Jesus. So when the rooster crowed that morning and Jesus's prediction had come true, Peter ran away in grief and humiliation.

"I think I will find him at the upper room," John said. "But I must go to him alone. If anyone goes with me, he will run away again. I must help him."

Clopas had joined us at the tomb, and he volunteered to accompany Jesus's mother, his wife, and me back to Bethany. "Go and join the rest of the apostles and women, and remain there for the Sabbath," John said. "No one should disturb you there, and you can then return here the following morning."

As we left the garden, we were passed by a detachment of Roman guards, whom we later learned were sent to guard the entrance to the tomb. We didn't give them much thought as we quietly made our journey to Bethany. None of us had any words of consolation for one another.

We silently reflected on the events we had seen and experienced. I knew if Jesus were with us, He would have told us to look to the Father and trust Him. And if Jesus had been there walking with us, it would have been easy to do that. But now without Him there, it was much more difficult!

When we arrived at the home of Lazarus, I was the one who told him, his sisters, and the apostles what we had witnessed that day. They experienced the same horror, disbelief, and grief we had.

A short time later, Andrew asked about Peter and John. When I told him what John had shared about Peter, Andrew became even more heartbroken. The fact that Judas had betrayed Jesus was one thing, but to learn that Peter had denied Him was quite another.

Each of us found a private place – either in the house or outside in the garden – to think about everything that had happened. I would like to say that one or two of us spoke up and reminded everyone of Jesus's promise to rise again. I wish I could tell you that Lazarus said, "Remember, He raised me from the dead. Surely, He, too, will return from the dead."

But no one did. We kept to ourselves and spent that Sabbath day wallowing in the depths of our despair – not standing on the assurance of hope.

The morning following the Sabbath, Salome, Joanna, Clopas's wife, and I waited until just before sunrise to leave Bethany and travel to where Jesus's body had been laid. Martha provided us with all of the ointments and perfumes we would need. She still had supplies from when they had prepared Lazarus's body for burial.

We were about halfway to the tomb when I realized the large stone covering the entrance would be too heavy for us to roll away. I have always been a stickler for details but had failed to consider this one in my grief. As always, though, the Father had been planning the details for eternity, and He had not forgotten anything!

When we arrived at the tomb, there was no sign of the Roman guards who had been posted. Surprisingly, we saw the huge stone had been rolled away. I immediately presumed someone had taken Jesus's body. Without even walking into the tomb, I left the other women and ran to alert John and Peter. I remembered John saying I would find them in the upper room.

When I arrived, the two men looked shocked to see me. "I was just leaving to go to the tomb to make sure you and the other women were able to roll away the stone," John said. "Were you able to move it? And have you already finished preparing Jesus's body?"

"No, we have not!" I cried out. "Someone has taken His body!"

"What do you mean, 'someone has taken His body'?" Peter asked. "Who would take His body?"

"The same people who had Him crucified!" I shouted back. "Perhaps the soldiers we passed last night took His body, or temple guards were sent to do so after the soldiers were called away. All I know is that when we arrived, the stone was rolled away and His body was not in the tomb."

"Mary, did you go inside the tomb and see that Jesus's body wasn't there?" John quietly asked.

"No, I didn't go in," I answered, somewhat embarrassed. It dawned on me that I should have looked inside, but I was so surprised the tomb was open, I hadn't given it a thought.

"Well, then," John replied, "let's go back and see."

We set off for the tomb. The two men ran much faster than I did, so Peter and John had already been to the tomb and were headed back toward Jerusalem when they met me still en route. They confirmed that His body was not in the tomb.

But John surprised me when he said, "He has risen!"

Risen? I had never considered that possibility. Could John be correct? I turned and looked at Peter. He didn't seem to be so sure.

"Do you remember what He said?" John asked. "He told us, '*The Son of Man is going to be betrayed into the hands of His enemies. He will be killed, but three days later He will rise from the dead?*'[1]

"Peter, do you think He has risen from the tomb?" I asked.

"I'm not sure what to think," Peter replied.

"Well, I am going to Bethany to tell Mary and the apostles that Jesus has risen," John declared. "They need to hear this good news!"

With that, he was off at a run. Peter started his walk back to the upper room at a slower pace. I wanted to believe John, but I wasn't convinced. I decided the only way I could know for sure was to return to the tomb – and go inside this time. So I continued in that direction, but this time my steps were a little quicker.

~

19

THE GARDENER

~

*W*hen I arrived back at the tomb and again saw the uncovered opening, the momentary spark of hope from my conversation with John quickly disappeared. It was replaced by my earlier doubt and fears. What had the religious leaders done with the body of my Lord?

The other women were no longer there. They had obviously returned to Bethany in distress. Suddenly, the tears I had been holding back burst forth. The idea that we, His closest friends and followers, were being robbed of the opportunity to properly prepare His body for burial, after all that had been done to Him, was more than I could bear.

I reached out and placed my hand on the outside of the cave to steady myself. But as soon as I touched the stone, a new thought came to me. Instead of the cold, unforgiving hardness of rock, the tomb somehow felt warm and inviting. It immediately reminded me of how I felt every time I was in the presence of Jesus. But how could that be?

I stooped down and peered inside the tomb. To my surprise, it was not empty! Two men, clothed in white, were sitting on the stone where Jesus's body had been laid. One was seated where His head should have been and the other where His feet would have been.

My appearance at the opening did not startle them; rather, they looked at me as if they had been expecting me. The man sitting at the head of the stone asked, *"Why are you crying?"*[1]

"Because they have taken away my Lord," I replied, *"and I do not know where they have put Him."*[2]

But before either of the men could respond, I sensed movement behind me. I glanced over my shoulder to see another man standing there. Unlike the first two men, He was not clothed in white. He most certainly wasn't a Roman soldier, nor was He one of the religious leaders. This Man was clothed in a plain cloak, more befitting a craftsman or a laborer.

I knew all of Jesus's close followers, so I knew He was not one of us. The only explanation was that He must be the tender of the garden.

He, too, asked, *"Why are you crying?"*[3]

But then He added, *"Who are you looking for?"*[4]

Surely, He must know whom I am looking for, I thought. If He is the gardener, He knows very well who has been laid in this tomb. And He must know where His body has been taken!

"Sir," I said, *"If You have taken Him away, please tell me where You have put Him, and I will go get Him."*[5]

The Gardener simply replied, *"Mary!"*[6]

The way He spoke my name shocked me more than the fact He knew it. Many people had called out my name during my lifetime. Most had done so as a greeting. It had often been done to gain my attention. My parents had done so during my childhood when I needed correction; but most often, they did so to express their love and affection for me. But only one Person had ever said my name in this way, and the first time was when He had set me free.

Immediately, the scales that had prevented my eyes from seeing Him fell away. I turned toward Him and exclaimed with joy, *"Rabboni!"*[7]

I moved to embrace Him. My Lord and Savior was alive! The One I had witnessed being crucified . . . the One I had seen die . . . now stood before me. And He was very much alive! I instantly thought of the day Jesus had called out to Lazarus to come out of the grave – and how we had all watched in awe as he did.

And now, Jesus Himself had walked out of His own grave! John was right – Jesus had risen! I could not contain my glee and excitement. My tears were suddenly transformed from sorrow to joy.

"Don't cling to Me," Jesus said to prevent me from embracing Him, *"for I haven't yet ascended to the Father. But go find My brothers and tell them that I am ascending to My Father and your Father, my God and your God."*[8]

I later discovered, as we all compared our accounts of His resurrection, that I was the first to whom Jesus appeared after He arose from the grave. It was an honor I will forever carry with me. But like all things my Lord has done for me – it was not an honor I ever deserved, but simply an honor He extended by His grace.

Soon after He appeared to me, Jesus appeared to my companions who had joined me earlier that morning as they headed back to Bethany. Jesus would then join Clopas and Shimon on their journey to Emmaus. They, too, would walk with Him for some time before their eyes were opened to see Him as their risen Lord.

Jesus also appeared to Simon Peter, so when we all came together that night in the upper room, he was no longer unsure what to think. He knew Jesus was alive!

Jesus told each of us that day to go find His other disciples and tell them that He had risen. He instructed us to tell them we were to gather in the upper room that evening, at which time He would appear before all of us.

I traveled back to Bethany that morning to tell those who were gathered at Lazarus's home. By the time I arrived, Salome, Joanna, and the wife of Clopas had already returned with their news. I could tell some of the apostles were still doubtful. But when I shared my account, distinctly separate from the others, more of the men began to believe us.

John had returned before all of us to tell Jesus's mother that He had risen. The two of them believed even before the other women and I had returned with our accounts. John and Mary had believed by faith; the rest of us had needed to see Jesus to believe. And later that night, all of us – except one – would have that same opportunity.

∽

20

THAT NIGHT IN THE UPPER ROOM

~

*L*ater that afternoon, those of us staying in Lazarus's home made our way to the upper room in Jerusalem. Even Lazarus and his sisters joined us on this journey. "I will not hide in my home out of fear," Lazarus told us. "If Jesus has risen from the dead, I have nothing to fear. Rather, it is those who want to harm me who should be fearful of God's judgment for what they have done!"

As I looked over our band of travelers, I realized we were all approaching the evening with different perspectives. Some of us had already seen Jesus and were looking forward to seeing Him again. Some, like Jesus's mother and John, had not yet seen Him but had faith they would see Him before the night was over. And then there were those who wanted to believe but still weren't certain.

But there was one who was not making the journey with us. The apostle Thomas had isolated himself from us since the day Jesus was arrested and crucified. When Thomas and the other apostles had arrived at Lazarus's home from the Garden of Gethsemane, Thomas had been so ashamed of his cowardice and abandonment of Jesus that he had refused to show his face. He had spent the past three days in Lazarus's vineyard and had refused to join the rest of us inside.

Even when Andrew told Thomas that Jesus was alive, he refused to come with us. "I do not believe it," he declared. "But even if I did, I could not face Him knowing that I ran away and left Him to fend for Himself."

"But we all did," Andrew had told Him. "You know as well as I do that we all have failed Him from time to time. And yet, He has always forgiven us. This time will be no different, Thomas. Come and see Him and receive His forgiveness."

But Thomas had refused and stayed behind.

When we arrived at the upper room, Simon Peter was already there. He excitedly told everyone how Jesus had appeared to him in that very room earlier in the day. As I looked around the room, I was surprised to see several men who had not been part of our group for these many months.

The Pharisees Joseph and Nicodemus were present. That made sense to me. After all, these men had boldly declared their belief in Jesus in front of their Sanhedrin brethren and had risked their positions and futures when they chose to claim and bury His body. News that Jesus had risen from the grave had spread quickly among the Sanhedrin, and the leaders were looking to squelch the news with rumors that we, His followers, had hidden His body. Joseph and Nicodemus had come that night to see Jesus with their own eyes.

The one who had carried Jesus's cross was also there. Simon had remained at the cross with us to the end and had been the one to carry Jesus's body to the tomb. It was fitting that he be here to greet the One in whom he had believed, even upon His death.

Several of us were stunned when Jesus's half-brothers – James, Joseph, Jude, and Simon – entered the room. Though we knew who they were, we also knew they had not been followers of Jesus. They were noticeably absent at His crucifixion. And I remembered how Jesus had given John charge of His mother as He hung on the cross.

But their mother had sent word to them through Clopas. Her message had been simply, "Your brother is alive! Come and see Him this evening!" She had included instructions on where we would be gathered. Oh, the thoughts that must have been running through their minds as they walked into that room! They all immediately went to their mother and embraced her, seeking her forgiveness for having abandoned her on a day when she needed them most.

As surprising as their appearance was, it paled in comparison to the one who arrived soon after them. Walking in behind Clopas and the shepherd Shimon was the criminal Barabbas. Jesus had been crucified on the cross that had been intended for him. The crowd gathered outside the praetorium in Jerusalem had been asked by Pilate whom he should pardon – Jesus or Barabbas. And the crowd had shockingly chosen Barabbas! In many ways, Jesus had borne Barabbas's penalty and death that day.

Seeing the apprehension on our faces, Clopas and Shimon helped Barabbas share his story of how he had come to believe in Jesus the very day Jesus had taken his place on the cross. As a matter of fact, Shimon told us Barabbas was the reason he and Clopas had journeyed to Emmaus that morning. They had gone to meet him and answer his questions about Jesus. And in the midst of their journey, Jesus had joined them.

As we listened to their testimony, I realized that Jesus had not only taken Barabbas's place on that cross – He had taken the place for all of us! I was thinking about that when all of a sudden Jesus appeared . . . out of nowhere!

And the door was locked! It was a good thing there weren't any large windows in the room, because otherwise I fear some of those who had not yet believed might have jumped out! They thought they were seeing a ghost. So, it was no wonder the first words Jesus said were, *"Peace be with you!"*[1]

Jesus calmed our fears and put us at ease. He ate a piece of broiled fish to assure everyone He wasn't a ghost. He showed us the wounds in His hands, His feet, and His side to prove He who was dead was now alive. The work the Father had given Him to do was now complete.

Gradually everyone's fear and anxiety turned to peace and joy! I watched as Jesus's eyes met with those of His half-brothers. The eyes of those who in many ways knew Him better than the rest of us; yet, they had refused to see Him for who He truly was. But now their eyes were opened to the truth. As the brothers returned His gaze, tears began to stream down the cheeks of all four men. Each fell to his knees and cried out, "Brother . . . Jesus . . . Master, forgive me!"

Then for a second time, Jesus said to us, *"Peace be with you."*[2] But this time it wasn't a word of peace for us in the room; it was a word of peace we were to go and share with a world that desperately needed peace. As the Father had sent Him, He was now sending *us.*

～

21

BACK IN MAGDALA

∿

*T*homas was with us when we were all back in the upper room one week later. When Jesus again appeared in our midst, He rebuked Thomas for his lack of faith – but I think it was also a reminder for each of us. At some point, we all had forgotten His promise and questioned His resurrection. All of us had experienced a testing of our faith.

As Peter reminded us many times after that day, Jesus in essence told us, "The world may say that 'seeing is believing,' but in the kingdom of God 'believing is seeing.'"

That night Jesus directed us to go to Capernaum and wait for Him there. It would give many of us the opportunity to see our families and tell them everything we had witnessed. Our journey would take us by Tiberias and Magdala.

Joanna decided to stop in Tiberias to see her family, and I decided to stop in Magdala to see my mother and brother. Joanna and I would travel on to Capernaum to join the rest two days later.

Though my mother saw Jesus as a Miracle Worker and a Good Teacher, she had not yet come to believe in Him as the Son of God. I hoped these most recent events would finally open her eyes.

Magdala was already abuzz with news of what had happened in Jerusalem. Most notably, the pilgrims who had returned from the Passover celebration reported how the crowd had embraced Jesus as the One sent by God. Actually, many of the pilgrims said they had gone to Jerusalem anticipating His arrival. Most shared they were certain the religious leaders would pronounce Him to be the promised Messiah, and He would lead our people out from under the yoke of foreign rule.

Many went on to tell how Jesus had then cleansed the temple the next day to the obvious dismay of the religious leaders. It was as if Jesus wasn't concerned about our Roman rulers as much as He was our religious leaders. Each day they had attempted to catch Him in a false teaching. But instead, He had revealed *their* false teachings. Though Jesus continued to perform miracles and teach in the temple for the next two days, it became obvious the religious leaders had no intention of declaring Him to be the Messiah.

The pilgrims went on to report that the religious leaders had conducted a secret trial in the middle of the night where Jesus was declared a threat to our people by teaching a message contrary to the law of Moses. To everyone's surprise, the leaders had then taken Him before the Roman prefect and accused Him of sedition. They demanded He be crucified. The One whom we had adored on Sunday had been crucified on Friday.

"Jerusalem is in an uproar," the pilgrims reported. "Some of His followers say Jesus has risen from the dead, but the religious leaders claim His followers have hidden His body. No one knows who to believe! Many of us have heard about the man He raised from the dead in Bethany, but could He really be able to raise Himself from the dead?"

My mother and brother had already heard these reports when I arrived at our home. After exchanging greetings, they began to question me. "Simon the Pharisee has already declared that those who followed Jesus are as guilty as He was," my brother began.

"He has warned the residents of Magdala to ignore the lies of His followers. He even named you specifically, saying, 'We all know Mary is a woman of ill repute and a disgrace to her family. She is representative of the type of people with whom Jesus surrounded Himself. If she is so bold as to return to Magdala, do not listen to her lies!'"

"His words do not surprise me," I replied. "We have all seen how Jesus and His teachings caused Simon to feel threatened – that his position of power and authority would suffer if we all turned to Jesus. He was more interested in protecting His control than He was in heeding the teachings of Jesus.

"Sadly that is true of most of our religious leaders. That is why they plotted against Jesus and arrested Him under the cover of darkness. Even the Roman prefect could find no reason to crucify Him but gave in to their political pressure. The forces of evil were truly at work – but they were not caused by Jesus, rather they were directed against Jesus. And if anyone knows the power of the forces of evil, I do!

"But those forces held no more power over Jesus than they did over me when He commanded them to leave me. That which was done to Him was only done because He permitted it. He taught us that the Father sent Him into this world to be the sacrifice for our sins. His blood was shed on that cross – not because of anything He did – but so the world through Him might be saved.

"Jesus taught, 'For God so loved the world that He gave His only Son, so that everyone who believes in Him will not perish but have eternal life.'"[1]

"But Mary," my mother interrupted, "what kind of a Savior can He be if He is dead?"

"He is not dead, Mother," I replied with a smile. "He is alive! He rose from that tomb. And I was the first person to see Him alive. I have seen Him with my own eyes – not on just one occasion but three different times. And so have many of us. The religious leaders have contrived this false rumor that we, as His followers, have taken His body and hidden it.

"There was a contingent of Roman soldiers guarding His tomb to keep that from happening. They have been bribed to remain silent about what they saw – and what they saw was Jesus walk out of that tomb!

"Adrianus, you are a man of business. If we took Jesus's body out of that tomb, where is His body now? And why haven't the religious leaders questioned any of us? They know what has happened and they are fearful!

"But the more important question to me, Mother, is what do you believe? Do you believe some dangerous Man delivered me from the very evil these religious leaders accuse Him of representing? Or do you believe He is the Son of the Living God, who has now risen from the dead?

"Sin has been conquered. Death has been defeated. You can no longer remain indecisive. Is Jesus who He said He was – or not? And if so, will you choose to believe in Him and follow Him today?"

~

22

A HILL OUTSIDE BETHANY

~

*T*hree weeks later, 120 of us gathered on the Mount of Olives outside Bethany, just as Jesus had instructed us. Forty days had passed since His resurrection, and for some of us, this was the fifth time we had been with Him. But as we gathered that day, Jesus told us He was going away. He was returning to His throne in heaven to sit at the right hand of the Father.

He assured us He would return again, but He didn't tell us when. He said only the Father knew when that day would be, but He also told us to live our lives in a way fully anticipating His return.

There were some among us who had known Jesus most, if not all, of their lives – like His mother and His half-brothers. There were a number who had known Him and followed Him between two and three-plus years, like the apostles and me. There were many, like me, who had begun to follow Him after He healed us, delivered us, or changed our lives through a miracle.

Some of us had been delivered from demons. Some had been blind, but now could see. Some had been paralyzed, but now could walk. Some had been dead, but now lived. Some had believed in Him for years. Some had come to believe in Him for only a few days. My mother was among that number.

Regardless of how long we had known Jesus, or how long we had followed Him, all of us stood on the hillside that day with a degree of sadness. We had become accustomed to being in His physical presence. We had become accustomed to hearing His voice and listening to His teaching. We had become accustomed to the peace of knowing we were in His presence.

We never needed to ask Him where we should go. All we ever needed to do was follow Him. As we stood on that hill, we knew this would be the last place to which we would follow Him – at least in His bodily form.

Jesus blessed us and said, *"I have been given all authority in heaven and on earth. Therefore, go and make disciples of all the nations, baptizing them in the name of the Father and the Son and the Holy Spirit. Teach these new disciples to obey all the commands I have given you. And be sure of this: I am with you always, even to the end of the age."*[1]

Then Jesus was taken up into the sky. We watched as He disappeared into a cloud. As we stood there, two white-robed men suddenly stepped out from among us. I hadn't noticed them before. I don't believe anyone had.

One of them said, *"Why are you standing here staring into heaven? Jesus has been taken from you into heaven, but someday He will return from heaven in the same way you saw Him go!"*[2]

I looked at them with a start. I recognized that voice. I had heard this man speak before. I studied the men's faces more closely, and I instantly recognized them. They were the two men I had seen sitting on the burial stone in the tomb. The one who had just spoken had talked to me that morning.

But then I realized I had seen them one other time. These were the same two men who had stood on the shore that day preventing me from walking into the sea to drown myself. They were the men who had delayed me long enough for me to encounter Jesus. I realized that every time I had seen them, they had somehow pointed me to Jesus – and they were doing it again.

The man who had spoken turned toward me and smiled. I now knew that Jesus had sent these men each time I needed to be delayed, or assured, or made aware. And now Jesus had promised He would send another who would guide us every step of the way.

Just before He ascended Jesus had also said, "*I will send the Holy Spirit, just as My Father promised. Stay here in the city until the Holy Spirit comes and fills you with power from heaven.*"[(3)] The One He was now sending would not be a being created by God; rather, it would be God's Spirit Himself.

As quickly as the two men had appeared, they disappeared. We all looked at one another. However, the Helper Jesus was preparing to send would never disappear. Once He came, He would be with us always.

After a few moments, I saw John look to the sky where Jesus had been, raise His hands, and begin to sing praises to His name. Soon, one by one, we all raised our hands and joined our voices with his in worship.

Eventually, Simon Peter and the rest of the apostles began to make their way to Jerusalem. Most of us followed them to the upper room where we met and prayed together for ten days.

On the tenth day, there was a sound from heaven that began like the roaring of a mighty windstorm. It filled the room where we were meeting. The Holy Spirit – the Helper that Jesus had promised – had now come upon us.

God had enabled us to watch and follow His Son as He taught and prepared us. Now, He had provided His Spirit to dwell within us to equip us to do all Jesus had taught us. Apart from the cross of Christ, we would still be separated from God by our sin. Jesus paid the price for the forgiveness of our sin! Apart from the Spirit of Christ, we would be incapable of living the life Jesus called us to live. His Holy Spirit living inside of us is what would make that possible!

And I knew it was time for me to go and live that life in the region He had placed before me.

~

23

THE GOOD NEWS SPREADS

~

*T*he next day several of us began our journey back to Galilee. Some of our number sensed the Holy Spirit's leading to remain in Jerusalem – including the apostles, Mary (the mother of Jesus), her sons, Mary (the aunt of Jesus), and Salome. The rest of us believed we were to return to our respective cities and bear witness to all we had seen and heard.

As we made our way through Galilee, our number began to dwindle as one-by-one members of our party remained in their respective cities. When we arrived in Tiberias, I bid my mother and brother farewell. Adrianus would be returning to his wife, Leila, his growing family, and the business that was now his to lead. My mother would be returning to her role as family matriarch and her more recent treasured role as grandmother. But in those roles, they, too, would continue to spread the Good News throughout Magdala and beyond.

I would not be continuing on with them to Magdala. The two of them would be far better suited to bear witness in that city. I, on the other hand, believed the Spirit wanted me to join Joanna in Tiberias. She and Chuza would continue to be a witness from Herod's palace, and my ministry would be in the heart of the city.

As I made my way along the city streets, I looked at the many buildings my family's business enterprise had built. I saw the rosettes carved into the cornerstones of each one. Once a symbol of personal pride and ambition, I now viewed them as a testimony to my Lord.

Jesus had taught us that He always had been – from before the beginning. He was there with the Father when the world was created. Our rosette had been designed to represent the six days of creation, but I now knew that it truly represented the Creator Himself – and the One who had been right by His side. Jesus is the rose – perfect in every way.

I momentarily felt guilty for the selfish ambition the rosette had once meant to me. But I was quickly reminded that my sin had been forgiven by the One who truly is the Rose. I prayed the knowledge of Him would now permeate the city.

I sought out the craftsmen and carpenters who had once been under my direction. One by one I told them about the Carpenter who had recrafted my life, and by God's grace several of the men came to believe in Jesus.

Chuza, Joanna, and I came together on the shore of the sea each Sabbath to pray and worship God. Each week more new believers joined us, as well as others who wanted to learn more.

One Sabbath day after we had been meeting for several months, I saw an old woman out of the corner of my eye watching from afar. I recognized who she was and approached her after our time of worship concluded.

"What brought you here?" I asked.

"I heard you were here, dearie, and I wanted to see how you were doing," she replied.

I knew that what had been done to me had not been done by this woman. It had been done by the evil spirit that dwelt within her. I spoke to the demon within her: "I command you in the name of Jesus Christ to come out of her!" Instantly it left her and the woman collapsed on the ground in front of me.

Joanna came over to join me and see what had occurred. The woman began to stir. The distant look in her eyes and her erratic speech were gone; instead, she was at peace.

"What happened to me?" the woman asked.

"You have been set free by Jesus Christ," I answered. "The one who has controlled you for so long no longer dwells within you."

"Where is this Jesus Christ? I would like to meet Him," she said.

I proceeded to tell her about Jesus – who He is, what He had done for me, what He had done for her, and what He had done for us all on the cross. By the time I was finished, she was ready to declare her belief in Him.

"What is your name?" I asked her.

"My name is Tabitha."

From that day forward, Tabitha grew in her faith in Jesus. She was baptized together with other new believers along the shore of the sea. The presence of the Spirit of God in her life was conspicuous to all those around her. As it turned out, she was an excellent seamstress who began to make clothing for the needy. Through her work, many came to believe.

Several months after she came to faith, Tabitha told me she needed to return to her home in Joppa along the Mediterranean Sea. "I have been away far too long, and I believe the Spirit of God would have me return there to tell others about Jesus," she said.

I was sad to see her go. Who would ever believe that the woman through whom I became controlled by demons would become my dear sister in the faith? But that's how the kingdom of God works. Jesus makes ALL things new!

Not long ago, I received news that Tabitha had become ill and died. The believers in her city sent for Simon Peter who was visiting nearby in Lydda. They led him to the room where her body was laid. By God's grace and through the power of His Holy Spirit, Tabitha was awakened from the dead. The same One who raised Lazarus has now raised Tabitha. The news has raced throughout the entire region, and many have believed in the Lord.

I am a witness of His greatness, His goodness, His grace, His mercy, His compassion, and His salvation. He delivered me from a life that was all about me and transformed me into a witness who is all about Him. I can no longer sit at His feet and anoint them with my tears as I once did. But I can worship Him as I minister to others as His hands and feet.

There were 120 followers that day on the hill outside of Bethany, but through the power of His Holy Spirit working through each of those witnesses, our number continues to multiply. I am told the religious leaders in Jerusalem are still trying to suppress the Good News of Jesus – but they will fail, just like they did when they tried to deny His resurrection.

Truth will always extinguish lies. Light will always put out the darkness. His name will always cause demons to run in fear. He is the One who has defeated death. Because Jesus is the Great I Am.

One day, I will again kneel at His feet and anoint them with precious perfume. But until then, I will remain . . . a witness called Mary.

∽

PLEASE HELP ME BY LEAVING A REVIEW!

i would be very grateful if you would leave a review of this book. Your feedback will be helpful to me in my future writing endeavors and will also assist others as they consider picking up a copy of the book.

To leave a review:

Go to: amazon.com/dp/1956866175

Or scan this QR code using your camera on your smartphone:

Thanks for your help!

~

YOU WILL WANT TO READ ALL OF THE BOOKS IN "THE CALLED" SERIES

Stories of these ordinary men and women called by God to be used in extraordinary ways.

<u>*A Carpenter Called Joseph*</u> (Book 1)

<u>*A Prophet Called Isaiah*</u> (Book 2)

<u>*A Teacher Called Nicodemus*</u> (Book 3)

<u>*A Judge Called Deborah*</u> (Book 4)

<u>*A Merchant Called Lydia*</u> (Book 5)

<u>*A Friend Called Enoch*</u> (Book 6)

<u>*A Fisherman Called Simon*</u> (Book 7)

<u>*A Heroine Called Rahab*</u> (Book 8)

<u>*A Witness Called Mary*</u> (Book 9)

<u>*A Cupbearer Called Nehemiah*</u> (Book 10)

AVAILABLE IN PAPERBACK, LARGE PRINT, AND FOR KINDLE ON AMAZON.

Scan this QR code using your camera on your smartphone to see the entire series.

"THE PARABLES" SERIES

An Elusive Pursuit (Book 1)

(releasing October 20, 2023)

Twenty-three year old Eugene Fearsithe boarded a train on the first day of April 1912 in pursuit of his elusive dream. Little did he know where the journey would take him, or what . . . and who . . . he would discover along the way.

~

A Belated Discovery (Book 2)

(releasing Spring 2024)

Nineteen year old Bobby Fearsithe enlisted in the army on the fifteenth day of December 1941 to fight for his family, his friends, and his neighbors. Along the way, he discovered just who his neighbor truly was.

~

For more information, go to *kenwinter.org* or
wildernesslessons.com

IF YOU ENJOYED THIS STORY ABOUT MARY ...

... you will want to read this novel about the shepherd Shimon

Shimon was a shepherd boy when he first saw the newborn King in a Bethlehem stable. Join him in his journey as he re-encounters the Lamb of God at the Jordan, and follows the Miracle Worker through the wilderness, the Messiah to the cross, and the Risen Savior from the upper room.

Though Shimon is a fictional character, we'll see the pages of the Gospels unfold through his eyes, and **experience a story of redemption – the redemption of a shepherd – and the redemption of each one who chooses to follow the Good Shepherd.**

AVAILABLE IN HARD COVER, PAPERBACK, LARGE PRINT, AND FOR KINDLE, AS WELL AS AN AUDIOBOOK ON AMAZON.

To order your copy:

Go to: amazon.com/dp/1732867097

Or scan this QR code using your camera on your smartphone:

ALSO BY KENNETH A. WINTER

THROUGH THE EYES
(a series of biblical fiction novels)

Through the Eyes of a Shepherd (Shimon, a Bethlehem shepherd)

Through the Eyes of a Spy (Caleb, the Israelite spy)

Through the Eyes of a Prisoner (Paul, the apostle)

∾

THE EYEWITNESSES
(a series of biblical fiction short story collections)

For Christmas/Advent

Little Did We Know – the advent of Jesus — for adults

Not Too Little To Know – the advent – ages 8 thru adult

For Easter/Lent

The One Who Stood Before Us – the ministry and passion of Jesus — for adults

The Little Ones Who Came – the ministry and passion – ages 8 thru adult

∾

LESSONS LEARNED IN THE WILDERNESS SERIES
(a non-fiction series of biblical devotional studies)

The Journey Begins (Exodus) – Book 1

The Wandering Years (Numbers and Deuteronomy) – Book 2

Possessing The Promise (Joshua and Judges) – Book 3

Walking With The Master (The Gospels leading up to Palm Sunday) – Book 4

Taking Up The Cross (The Gospels – the passion through ascension) – Book 5

Until He Returns (The Book of Acts) – Book 6

ALSO AVAILABLE AS AUDIOBOOKS

THE CALLED

(the complete series)

A Carpenter Called Joseph

A Prophet Called Isaiah

A Teacher Called Nicodemus

A Judge Called Deborah

A Merchant Called Lydia

A Friend Called Enoch

A Fisherman Called Simon

A Heroine Called Rahab

A Witness Called Mary

A Cupbearer Called Nehemiah

∼

Through the Eyes of a Shepherd

∼

Little Did We Know

Not Too Little to Know

∼

SCRIPTURE BIBLIOGRAPHY

~

The basis for the story line of this book is taken from the Gospels.
Certain fictional events or depictions of those events have been added.

Some of the dialogue in this story are direct quotations from Scripture.
Here are the specific references for those quotations:

Preface

[1] 1 Corinthians 1:26-29

[2] Luke 8:2

Chapter 1

[1] Luke 7:39

[2] Luke 7:40-42

[3] Luke 7:43

[4] Luke 7:43

[5] Luke 7:44-47

(6) Luke 7:48, 50

Chapter 3

(1) Proverbs 24:27 (NASB)

Chapter 4

(1) Proverbs 18:22 (NASB)

(2) Proverbs 16:11, 13 (ESV)

Chapter 11

(1) Luke 7:48, 50

(2) Luke 7:50

Chapter 12

(1) John 11:43

Chapter 13

(1) John 12:5

(2) Mark 14:6

(3) Matthew 21:9

(4) Luke 1:32-33

(5) Luke 19:39

(6) Luke 19:40

(7) Matthew 21:9

Chapter 14

[1] John 13:6

[2] John 13:7

[3] John 13:8a

[4] John 13:8b

[5] John 13:9

[6] John 13:10

[7] Luke 22:19

[8] Luke 22:20, 17-18

Chapter 15

[1] Mark 14:45

[2] Luke 22:48

[3] Luke 22:51; Matthew 26:52-53

[4] Luke 22:52-53; John 18:8

Chapter 16

[1] Luke 23:28

[2] John 19:26-27

[3] John 8:12

Chapter 17

[1] John 19:30

Chapter 18

[1] Mark 9:31

Chapter 19

[1] John 20:13a

[2] John 20:13b

[3] John 20:15a

[4] John 20:15b

[5] John 20:15c

[6] John 20:16a

[7] John 20:16b

[8] John 20:17

Chapter 20

[1] John 20:19

[2] John 20:21

Chapter 21

[1] John 3:16

Chapter 22

[1] Matthew 28:18-20

[2] Acts 1:11

[3] Luke 24:49

Unless otherwise indicated, all Scripture quotations are taken from the *Holy Bible*, New Living Translation, copyright © 1996. Used by permission of Tyndale House Publishers, Inc., Wheaton, Illinois 60189. All rights reserved.

Scripture quotations marked (NASB) are taken from the *New American Standard Bible*, copyright © 1960, 1962, 1963, 1968, 1971, 1972, 1973, 1975,

1977 by The Lockman Foundation, La Habra, California. All rights reserved.

Scripture quotations marked (ESV) are taken from *The Holy Bible, English Standard Version*, copyright © 2001 by Crossway, a publishing ministry of Good News Publishers. Used by permission. All rights reserved.

〜

LISTING OF CHARACTERS
(ALPHABETICAL ORDER)

∿

Many of the characters in this book are real people pulled directly from the pages of Scripture — most notably Jesus! i have not changed any details about a number of those individuals — again, most notably Jesus — except the addition of their interactions with the fictional characters. They are noted below as "UN" (unchanged).

In other instances, fictional details have been added to real people to provide backgrounds about their lives where Scripture is silent. The intent is that you understand these were real people, whose lives were full of all of the many details that fill our own lives. They are noted as "FB" (fictional background).

In some instances, we are never told the names of certain individuals in the Bible. In those instances, where i have given them a name as well as a fictional background, they are noted as "FN" (fictional name).

Lastly, a number of the characters are purely fictional, added to convey the fictional elements of these stories. They are noted as "FC" (fictional character).

∽

Adrianus – Greek name of Lemuel
Andrew – son of Jonah, brother of Simon Peter, apostle of Jesus (FB)
Annas – high priest (6 - 15 A.D.) (FB)
Barabbas – criminal released by Pontius Pilate (FB)
Bartholomew – fisherman, apostle of Jesus (UN)
Caiaphas – high priest (18 - 36 A.D.) (FB)
Chuza – Herod's steward, husband of Joanna (FB)
Clopas – brother of Joseph, earthly uncle of Jesus, father of James (the less) & Thaddeus (FB)
Galenka – wife of Jacob, mother of Mary and Lemuel (Adrianus) (FC)
Herod Antipas – 6th son of Herod the Great, puppet king who ruled Galilee (2 B.C - 39 A.D.) (FB)
Herod Archelaus – 5th son of Herod the Great, puppet king who ruled Iudaea (2 B.C - 6 A.D.) (UN)
Herod the Great – the tetrarch (37 - 2 B.C.) (UN)
Ishmael – son of Shebna, father of Salome (FC)
Jacob – husband of Galenka, father of Mary & Lemuel (Adrianus) (FC)
James – son of Joseph & Mary, half-brother of Jesus (UN)
James – son of Zebedee, brother of John, apostle of Jesus (FB)
James (the Less) – son of Clopas, cousin of Jesus, apostle of Jesus (FB)
Jesus of Nazareth – the Son of God (UN)
Joanna – wife of Chuza (FB)
Johanan – father of Jacob, grandfather of Mary & Lemuel (Adrianus) (FC)
John – son of Zebedee, brother of James, apostle of Jesus (FB)
Joseph (of Arimathea) – Pharisee (FB)
Joseph (of Nazareth) – husband of Mary, earthly father of Jesus (UN)
Joseph (son of Joseph) – son of Joseph & Mary, half-brother of Jesus (UN)
Judas Iscariot – the betrayer (FB)
Jude – son of Joseph & Mary, half-brother of Jesus (UN)
Lazarus – brother of Martha & Mary, raised from the dead by Jesus (FB)
Leila – wife of Lemuel (Adrianus) ((FC)
Lemuel (Adrianus) – son of Jacob & Galenka, brother of Mary, husband of Leila (FC)
Martha – sister of Lazarus & Mary (Miriam) (FB)

Mary (of Magdala) – daughter of Jacob & Galenka, sister of Lemuel (Adrianus) (FB)

Mary (of Nazareth) – mother of Jesus, wife of Joseph (FB)

Mary (wife of Clopas) – mother of James (the less) & Thaddeus (FB)

Mathias – Jacob's partner in fishery in Magdala (FC)

Matthew – apostle of Jesus, former tax collector (UN)

Miriam – sister of Lazarus & Martha (FB)

Nicodemus – rabbi in Capernaum - pharisee & disciple of Jesus (FB)

Philip – fisherman, apostle of Jesus (FB)

Pontius Pilate – 5th Roman prefect of Iudaea (FB)

Salome – daughter of Ishmael, wife of Zebedee, mother of James & John (FB)

Shebna – brother of Hillel, father of Ishmael (FC)

Shimon – shepherd, disciple of John the baptizer, disciple of Jesus (FC)

Simon (son of Joseph) – son of Joseph & Mary, half-brother of Jesus (UN)

Simon (the Cyrene) – carried the cross of Jesus (FB)

Simon (the Pharisee) – Pharisee living in Magdala (FB)

Simon (the zealot) – apostle of Jesus (FB)

Simon Peter – son of Jonah, apostle of Jesus (FB)

Susanna – grieving mother whose son was raised from the dead (FN)

Tabitha – woman in Tiberias who later moves to Joppa (FB)

Thaddeus – son of Clopas, cousin of Jesus, apostle of Jesus (FB)

Thomas – son of Eber, twin brother of Gabriella, apostle of Jesus (FB)

Unnamed men dressed in white – angels (FB)

Unnamed servant of Simon the Pharisee (FC)

Yitzhak – the tradesman who owned the upper room (FC)

Zebedee – husband of Salome, father of James and John (FB)

❧

ACKNOWLEDGMENTS

I do not cease to give thanks for you ....
Ephesians 1:16 (ESV)

... my partner and best friend, LaVonne,
for choosing to trust God as we walk with Him in this faith adventure;

... my family,
for your continuing love, support and encouragement;

... Sheryl,
for your partnership in the work;

... Scott,
for using the gifts God has given you;

... a precious group of advance readers,
who encourage and challenge me in the journey;

... and most importantly,
the One who goes before me in all things
– my Lord and Savior Jesus Christ!

∾

FROM THE AUTHOR

A word of explanation for those of you who are new to my writing.

∾

You will notice that whenever i use the pronoun "I" referring to myself, i have chosen to use a lowercase "i." This only applies to me personally (in the Preface). i do not impose my personal conviction on any of the characters in this book. It is not a typographical error. i know this is contrary to proper English grammar and accepted editorial style guides. i drive editors (and "spell check") crazy by doing this. But years ago, the Lord convicted me – personally – that in all things i must decrease and He must increase.

And as a way of continuing personal reminder, from that day forward, i have chosen to use a lowercase "i" whenever referring to myself. Because of the same conviction, i use a capital letter for any pronoun referring to God throughout the entire book. The style guide for the New Living Translation (NLT) does not share that conviction. However, you will see that i have intentionally made that slight revision and capitalized any pronoun referring to God in my quotations of Scripture from the NLT. If i have violated any style guides as a result, please accept my apology, but i must honor this conviction.

Lastly, regarding this matter – this is a <u>personal</u> conviction – and i share it only so you will understand why i have chosen to deviate from normal editorial practice. i am in no way suggesting or endeavoring to have anyone else subscribe to my conviction. Thanks for your understanding.

∾

ABOUT THE AUTHOR

Ken Winter is a follower of Jesus, an extremely blessed husband, and a proud father and grandfather – all by the grace of God. His journey with Jesus has led him to serve on the pastoral staffs of two local churches – one in West Palm Beach, Florida and the other in Richmond, Virginia – and as the vice president of mobilization of the IMB, an international missions organization.

Today, Ken continues in that journey as a full-time author, teacher and speaker. You can read his weekly blog posts at kenwinter.blog and listen to his weekly podcast at kenwinter.org/podcast.

❧

And we proclaim Him, admonishing every man and teaching every man with all wisdom, that we may present every man complete in Christ. And for this purpose also I labor, striving according to His power, which mightily works within me.
(Colossians 1:28-29 NASB)

PLEASE JOIN MY READERS' GROUP

Please join my Readers' Group in order to receive updates and information about future releases, etc.

Also, i will send you a free copy of *The Journey Begins* e-book — the first book in the *Lessons Learned In The Wilderness* series. It is yours to keep or share with a friend or family member that you think might benefit from it.

It's completely free to sign up. i value your privacy and will not spam you. Also, you can unsubscribe at any time.

Go to kenwinter.org to subscribe.

Or scan this QR code using your camera on your smartphone:

∼

Made in the USA
Thornton, CO
09/07/23 11:55:57

95215d8c-b61f-423d-9df0-2114204f2bc6R01